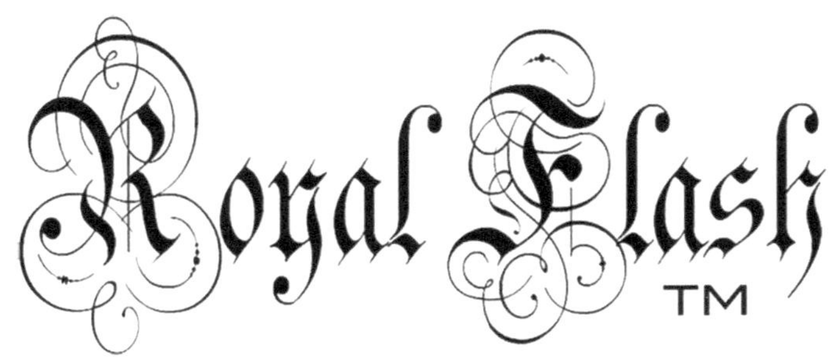

Presents

"Colossal Color"

All Artwork by

Cort Bengtson

Published by
Corts Royal Ink Tattoo Company
Book Design and Layout by Cort Bengtson

Foward

This is a collection of tattoo art from American born Artist Cort Bengtson that represents things from nature and of fiction done in the mixing of tattoo styles such as Japanese, American traditional and newschool.

It was all Hand drawn in about a 2 month period using micron pens on plain white paper and then scanned and colored in completely on computer using a 22" drawing tablet and Photoshop.

Some things were easier and some things were a little more generic and clumbsy until I got the hang of adjusting the brush presets on the fly.

Conclusion? I am definitely not ready to give up traditional drawing and coloring means. Your hands still do so many things intuitively that the computer doesn't think to do. The tooth of the paper is most missed drawing on the tablet screen. If You can get used to that,you'll love using a tablet. Some tattooist respect the hand drawn aspect as core to the profession of tattooing and don't like the idea of using the computer for anything.. But after tattooing for more than 20 years I can honestly say using the computer and drawing tablet presents it's own challenges and has it's own learning aspects. And allows you to try differnt things that you can bring back to tattooing.

On the plus side, the smooth blends and big coverage happen so fast it actually speeds up the time it takes to do something so much so that your learning process speeds up by ten fold. Did someone say faster learning.?And the computer gives as many redos and erasing as we want. So you can try things you might not risk on a client's tattoo.

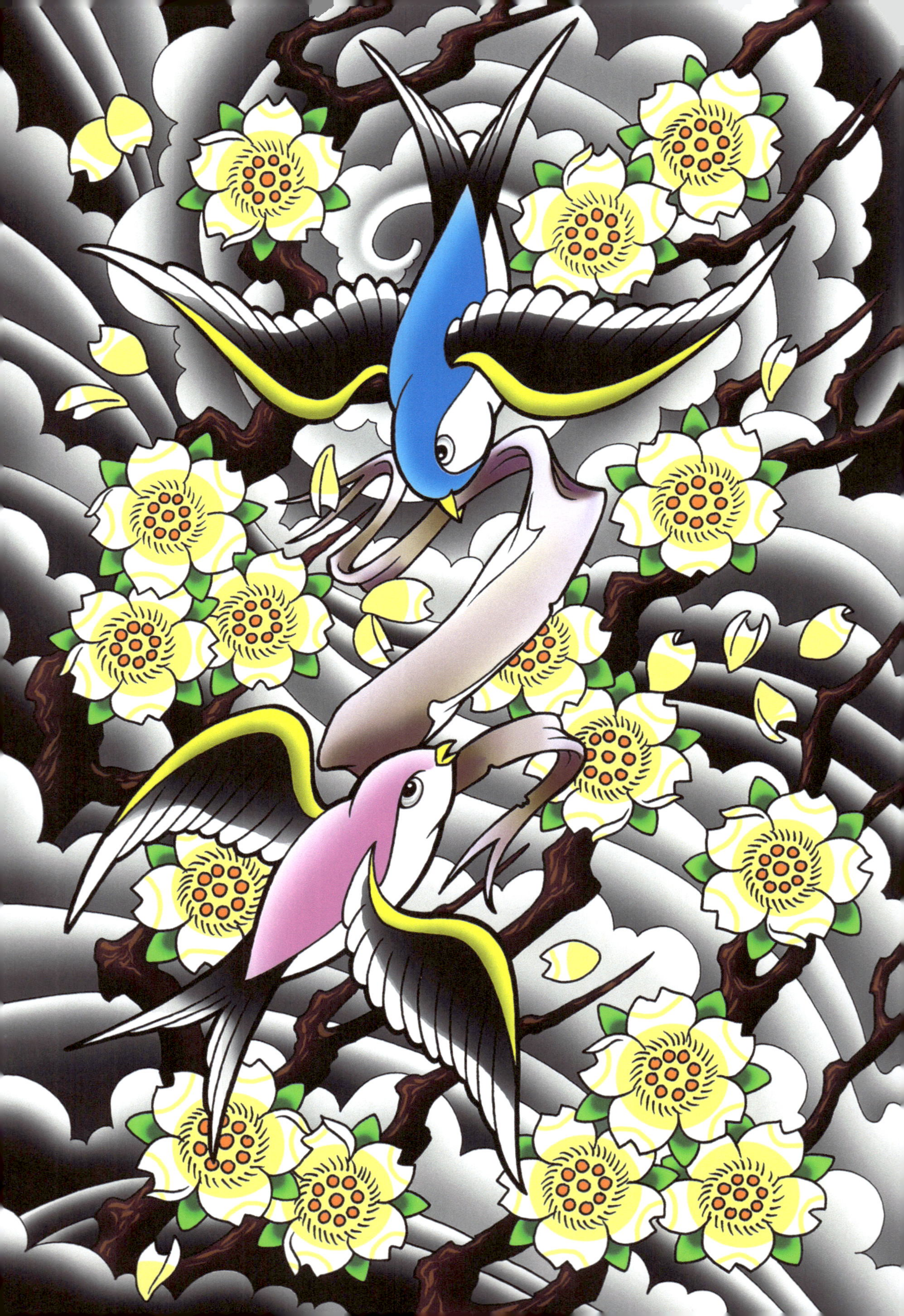

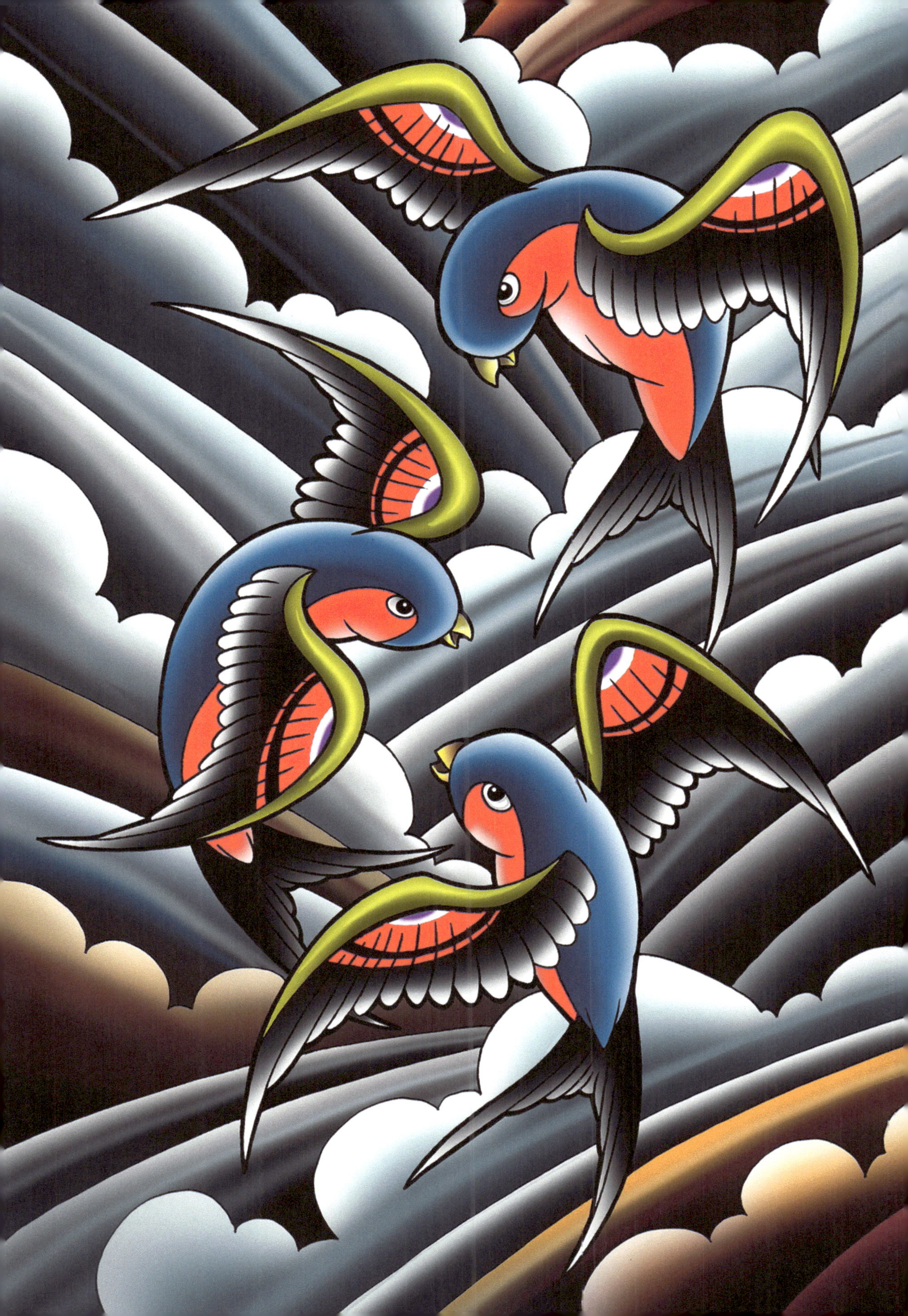

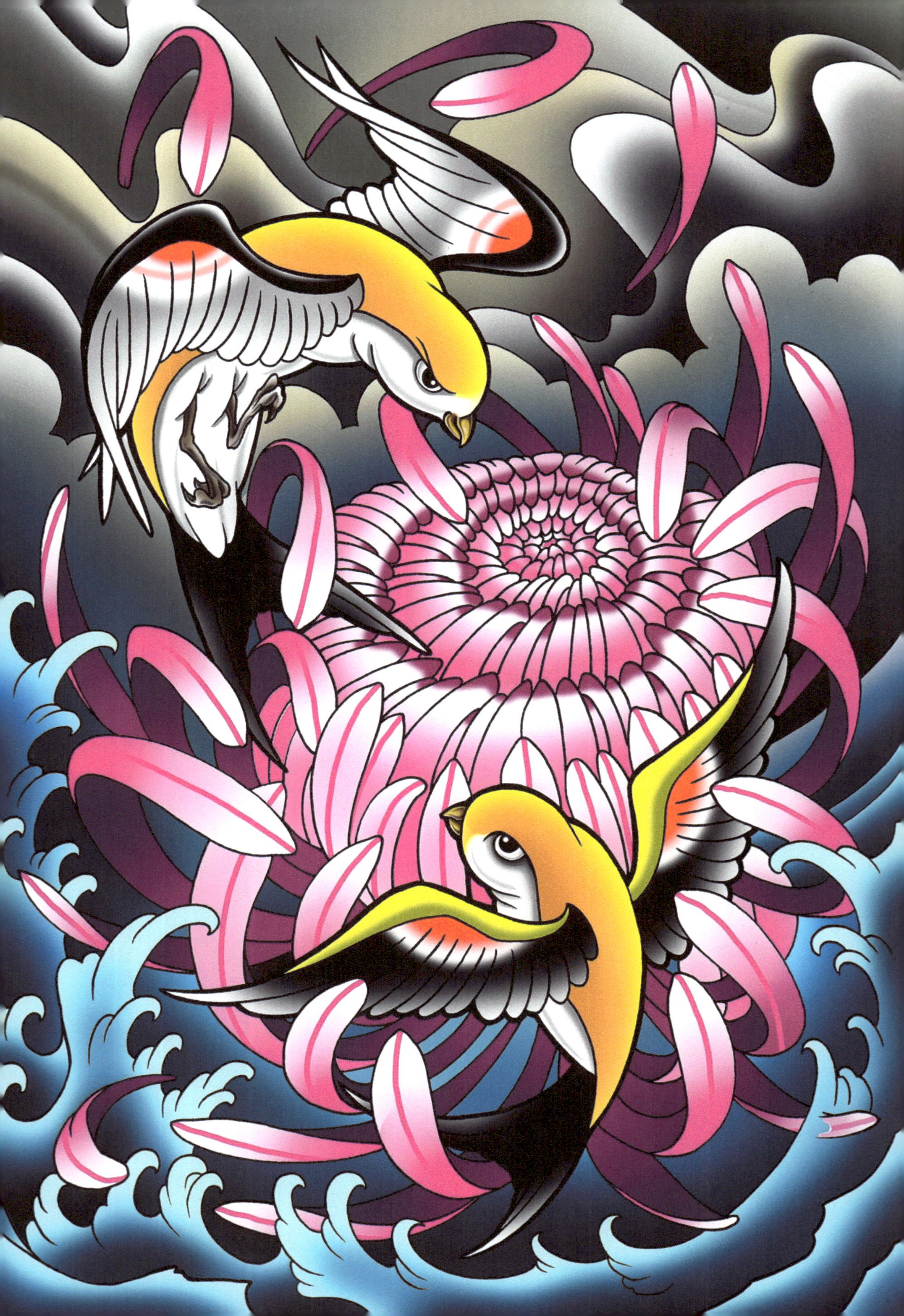

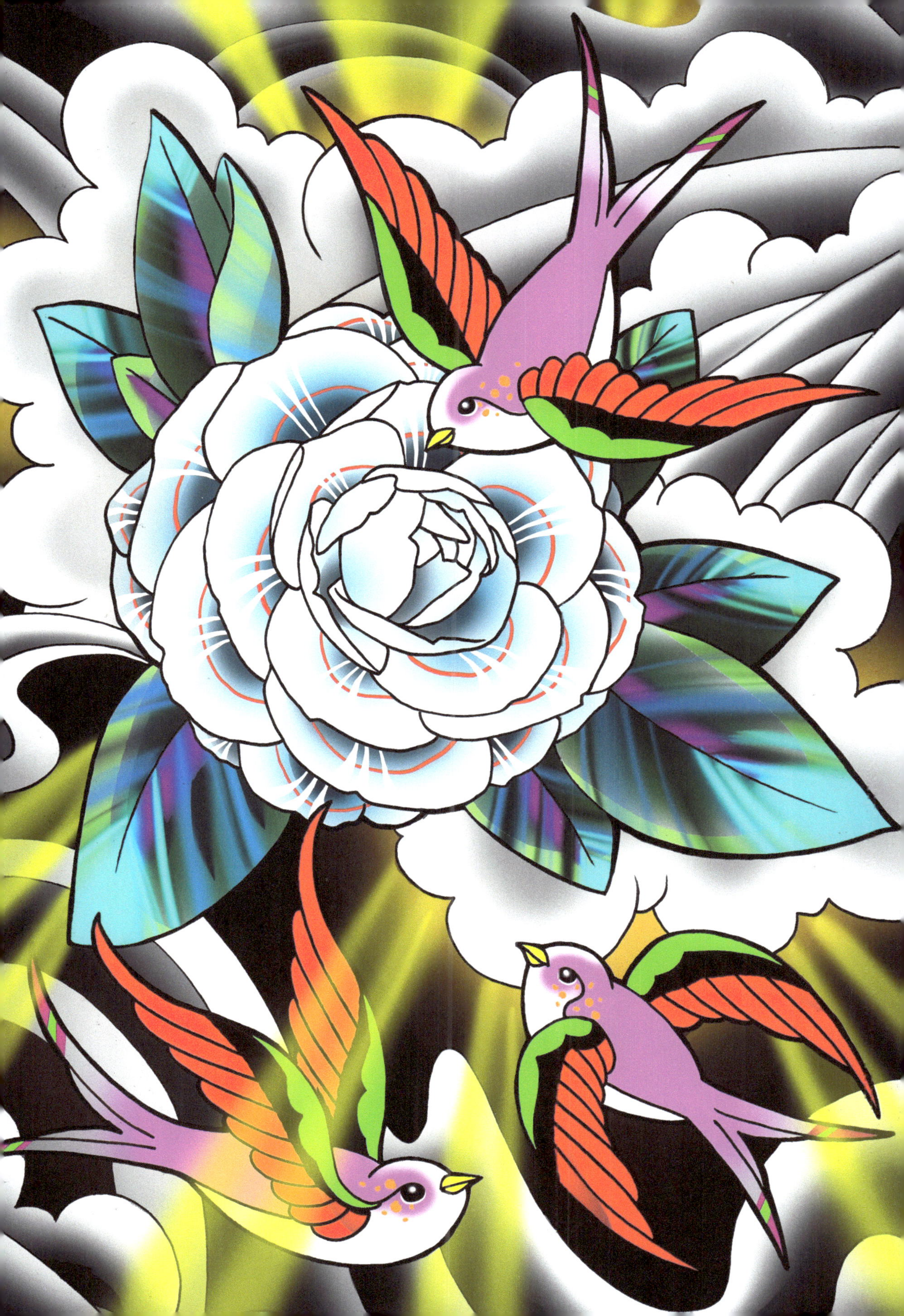

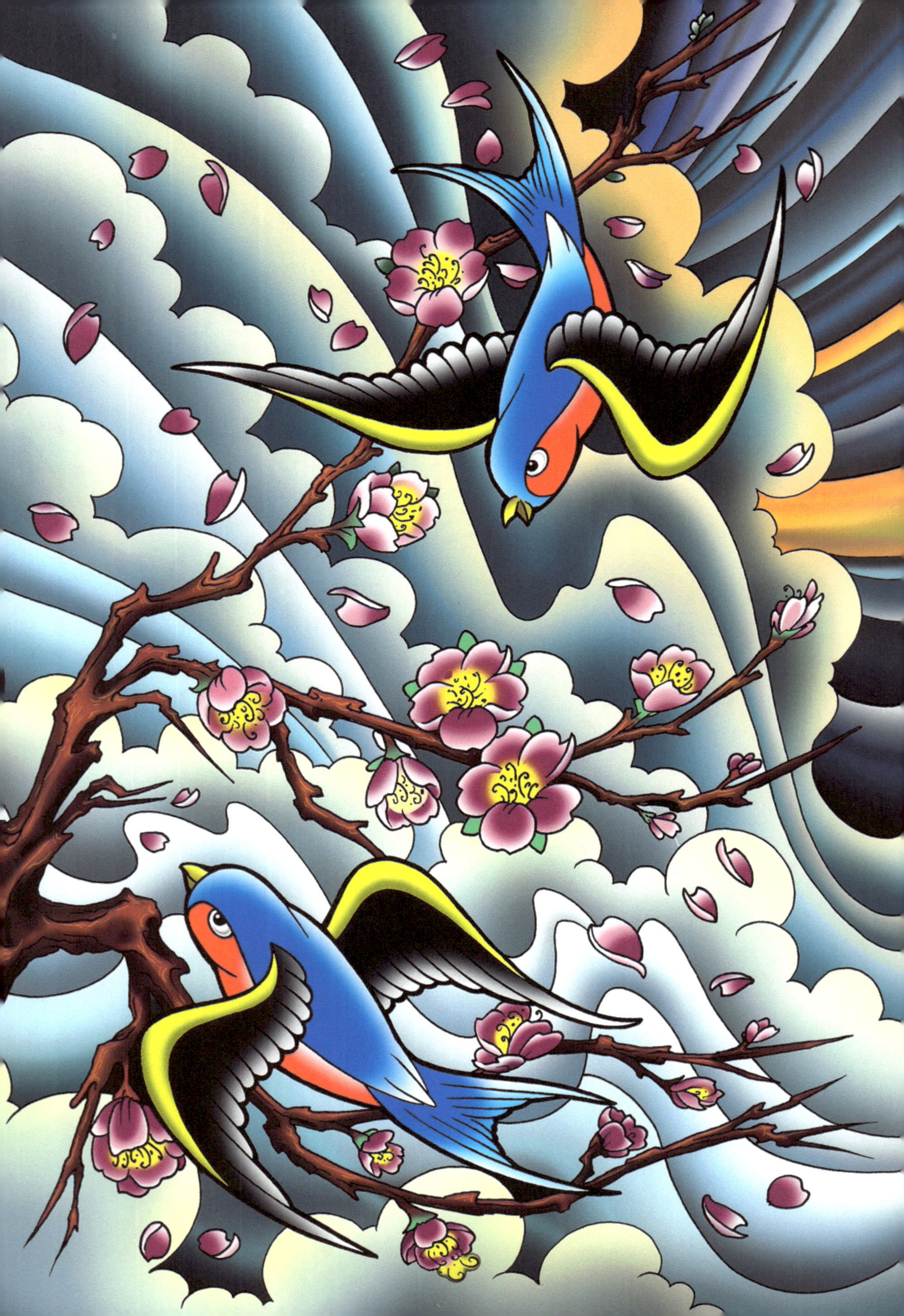

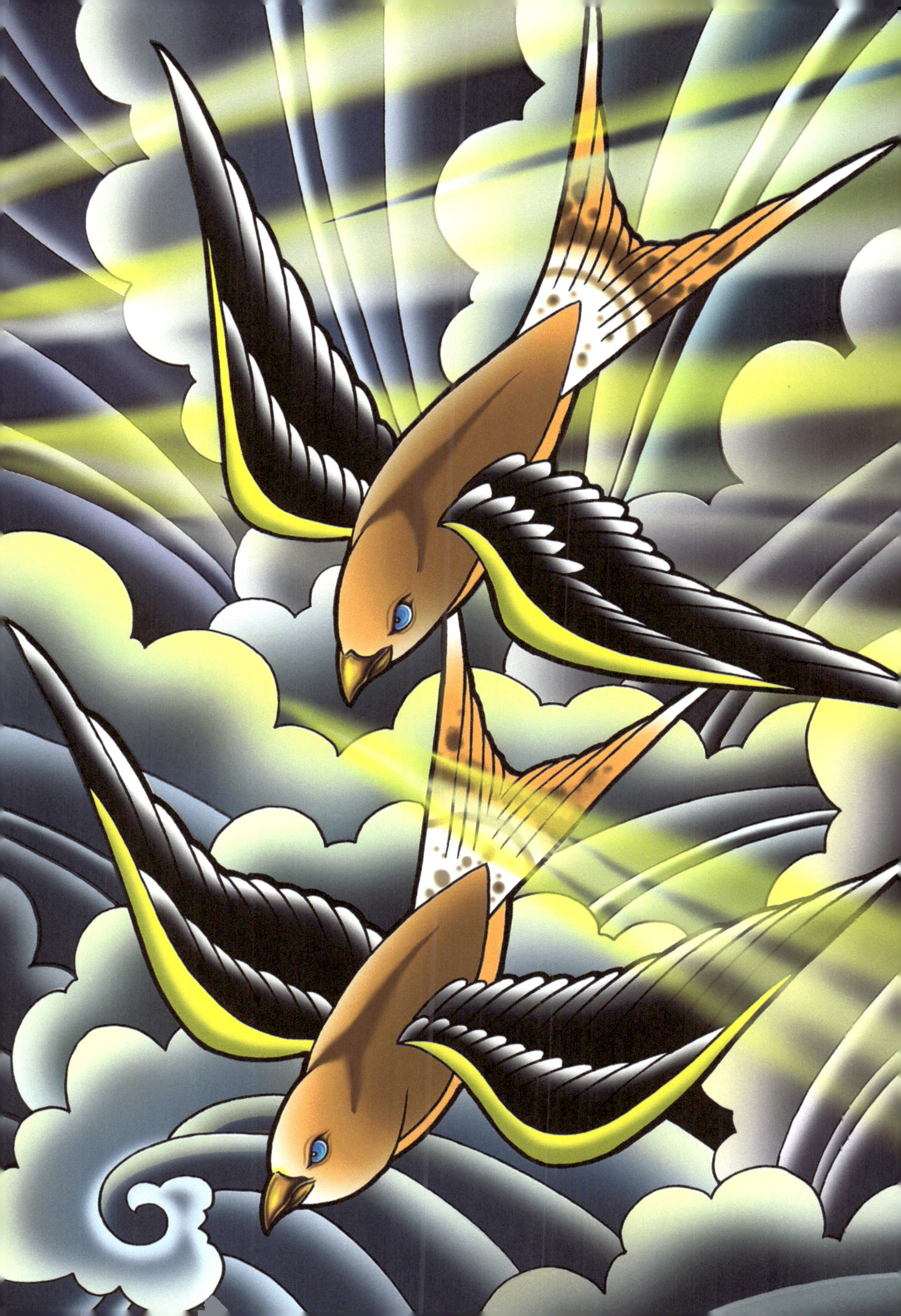

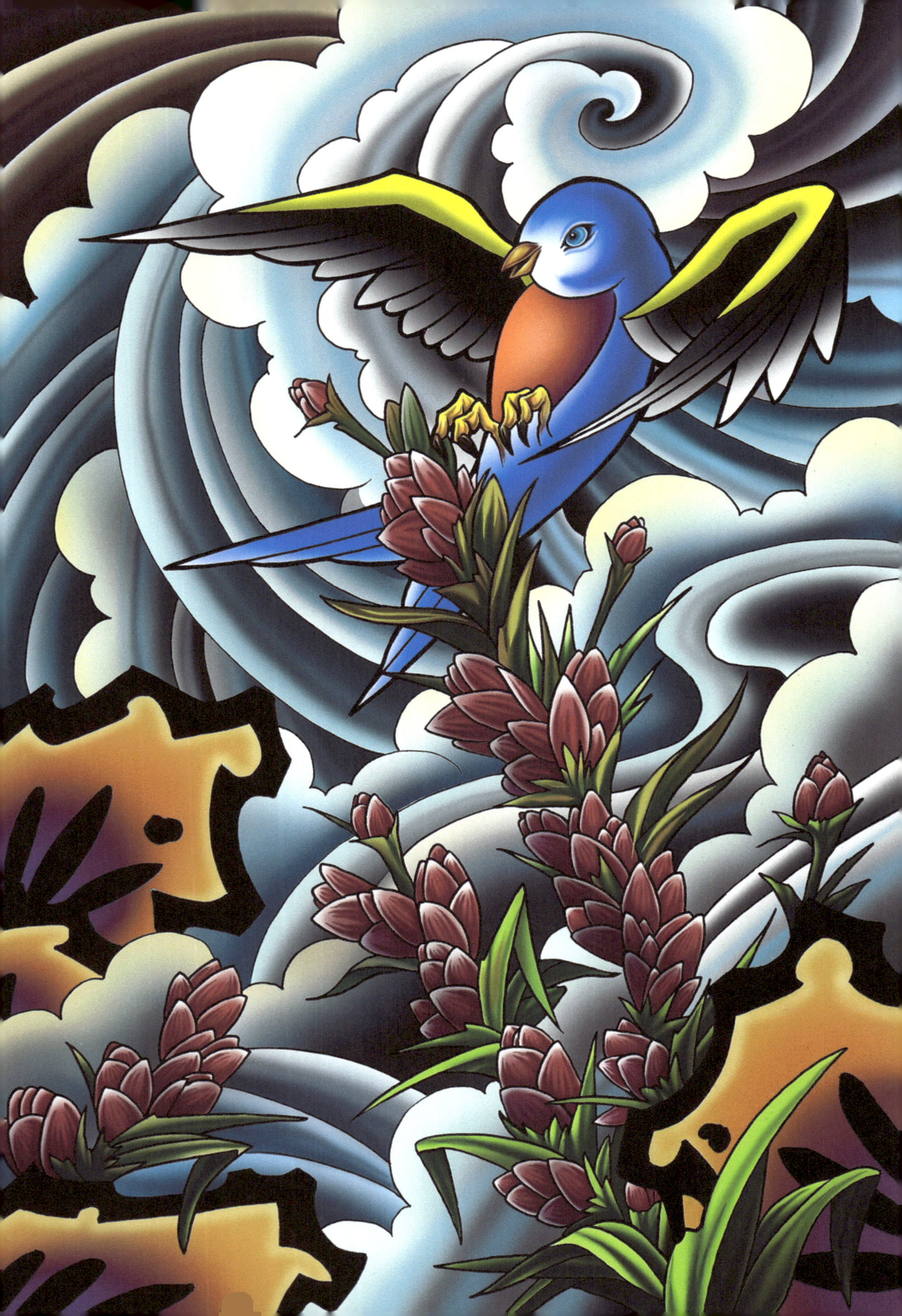

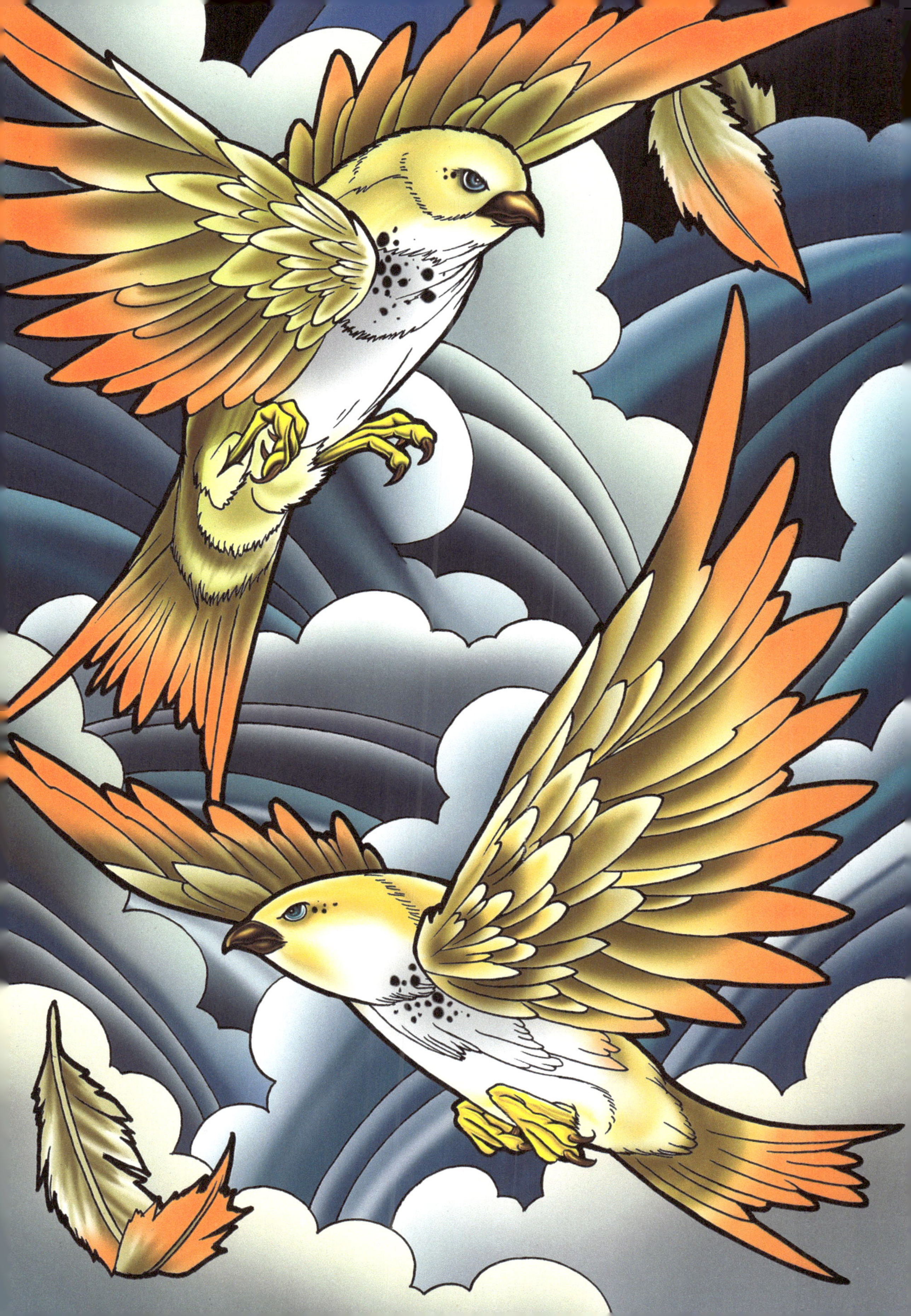

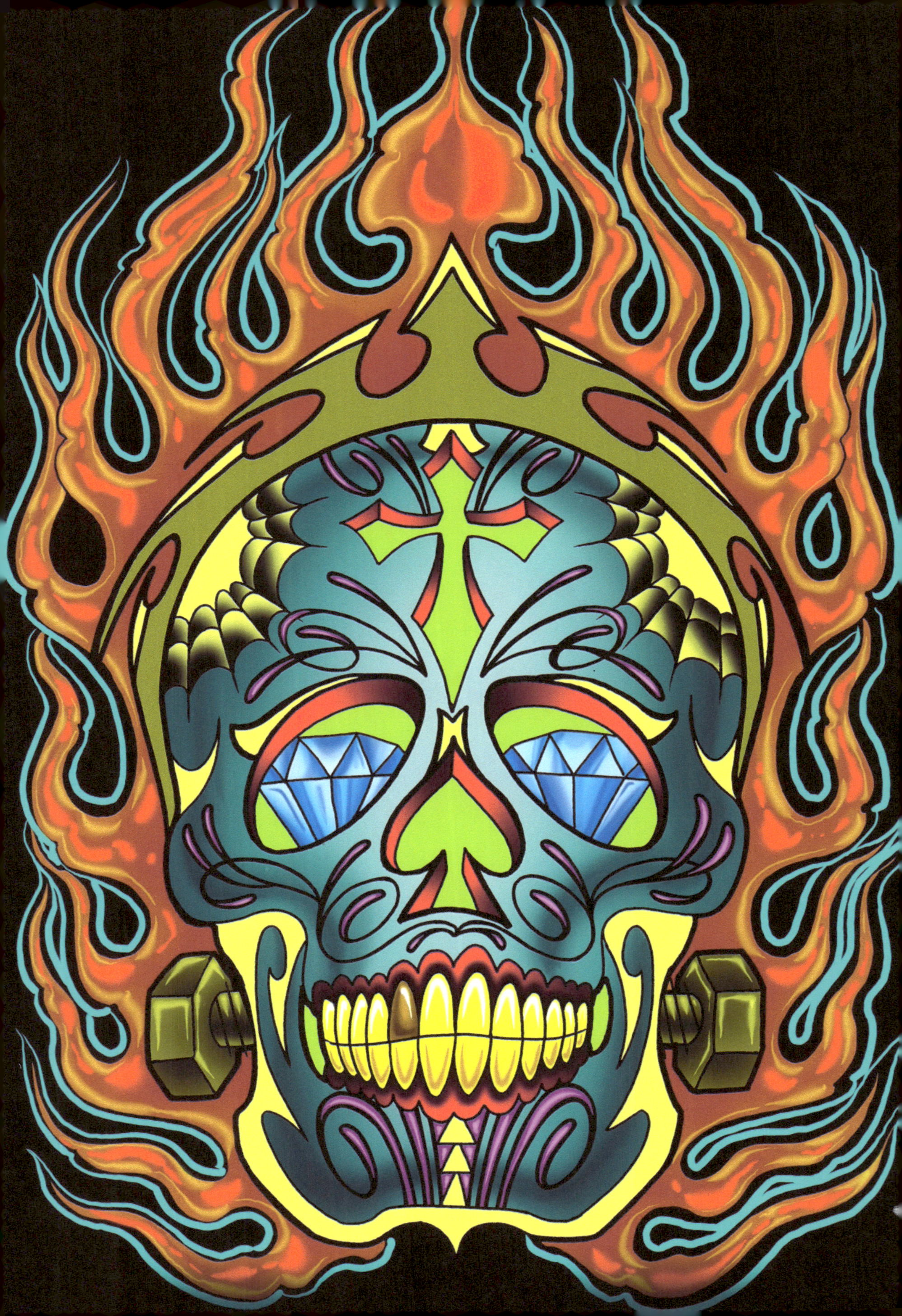

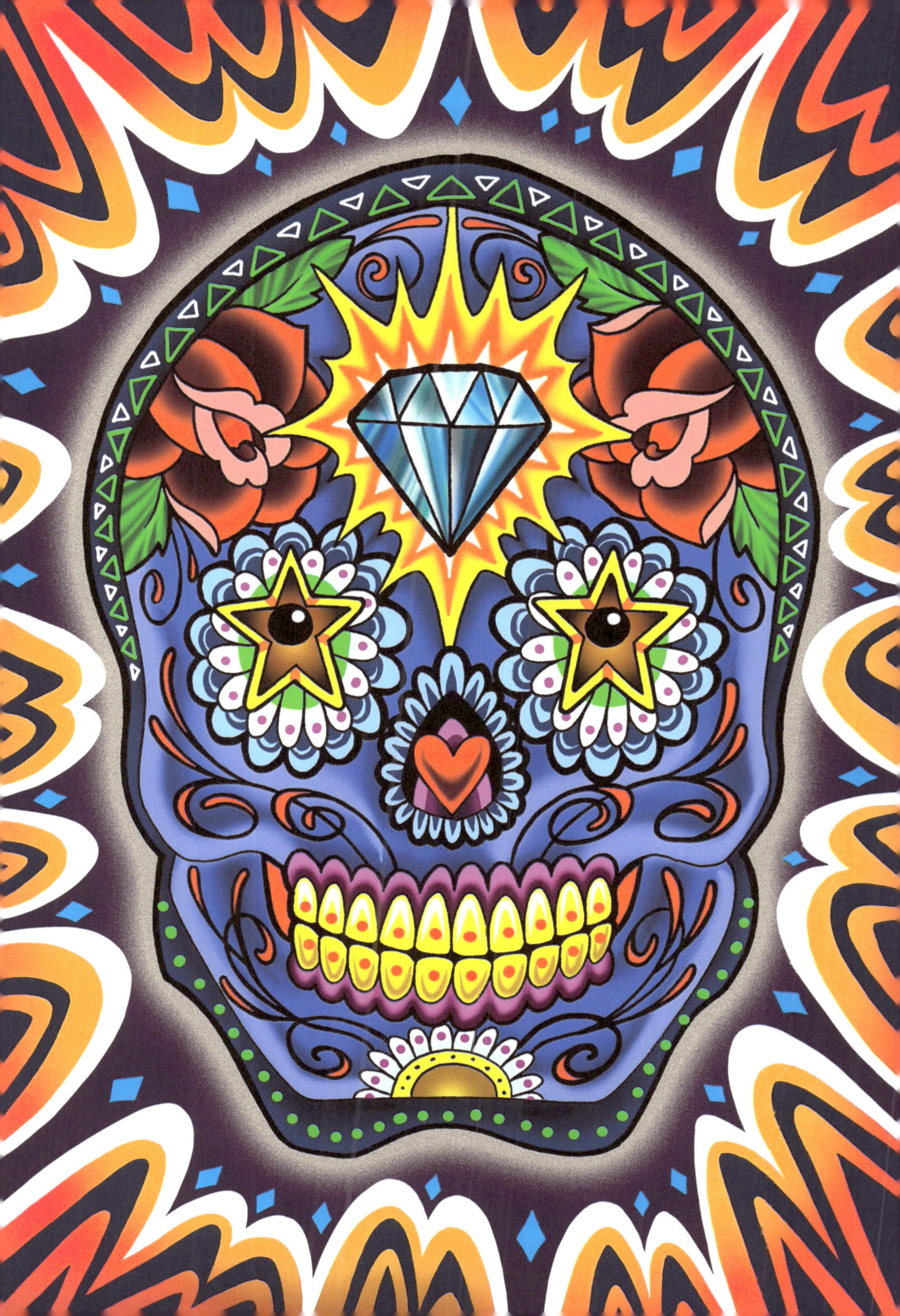

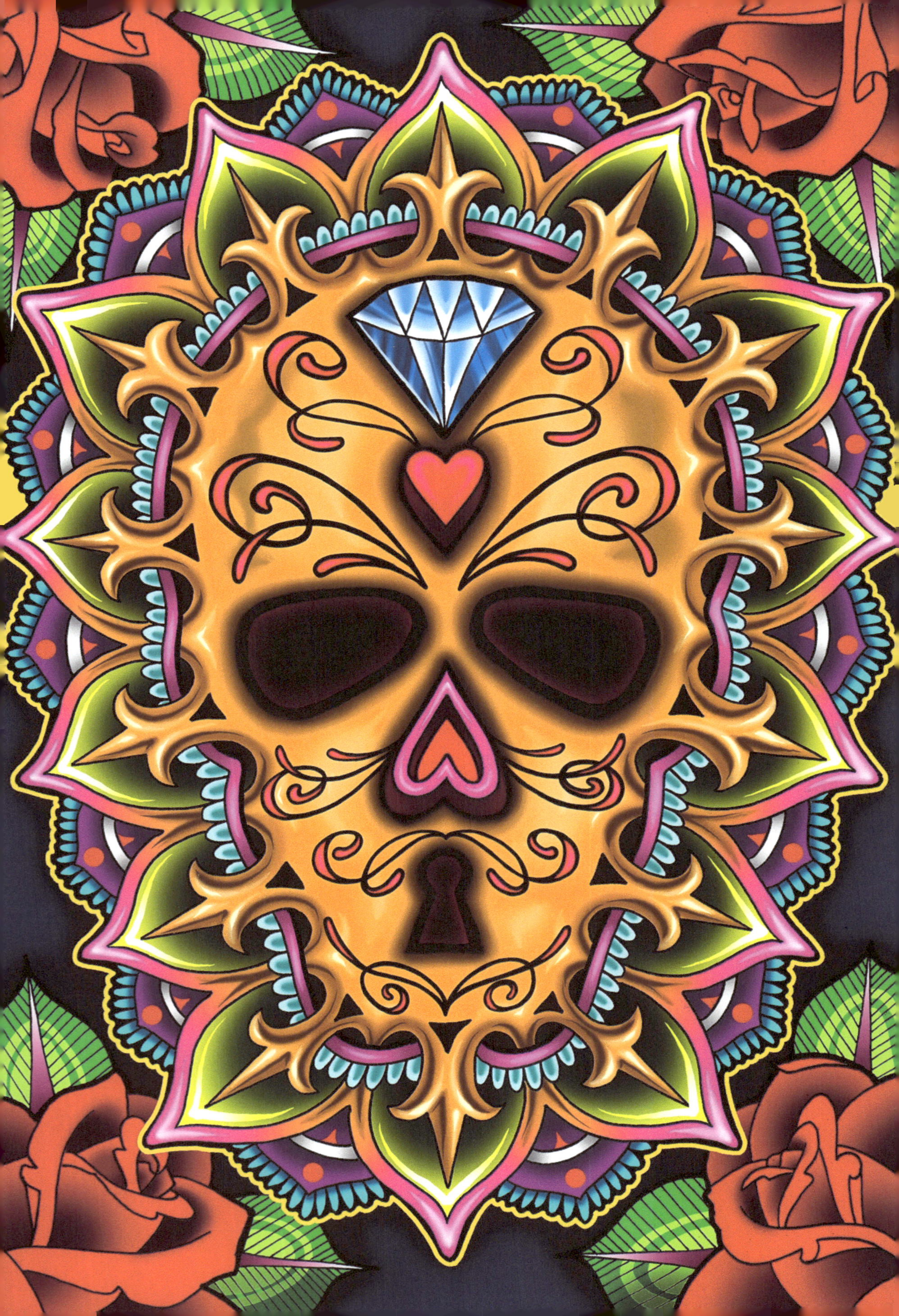

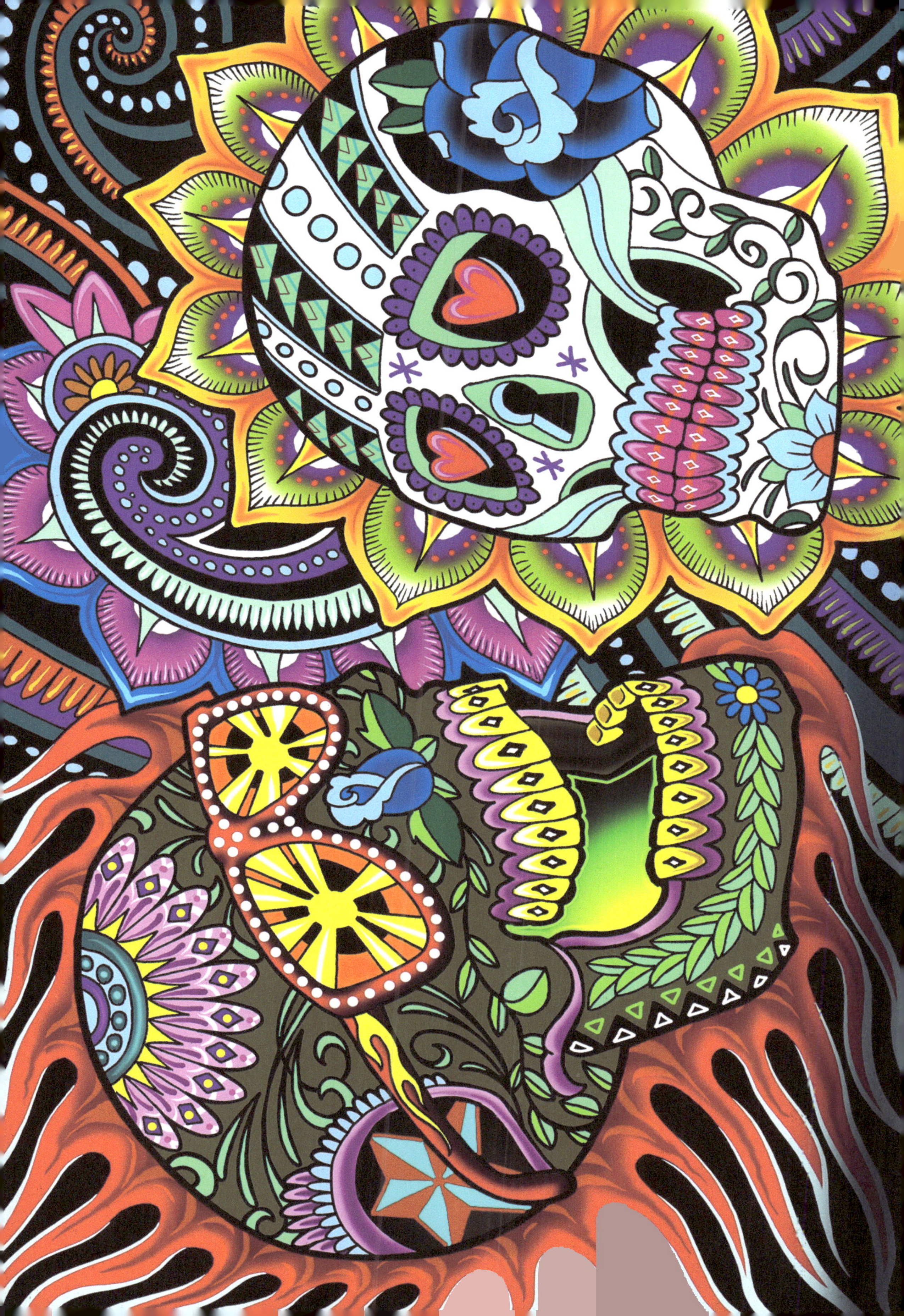

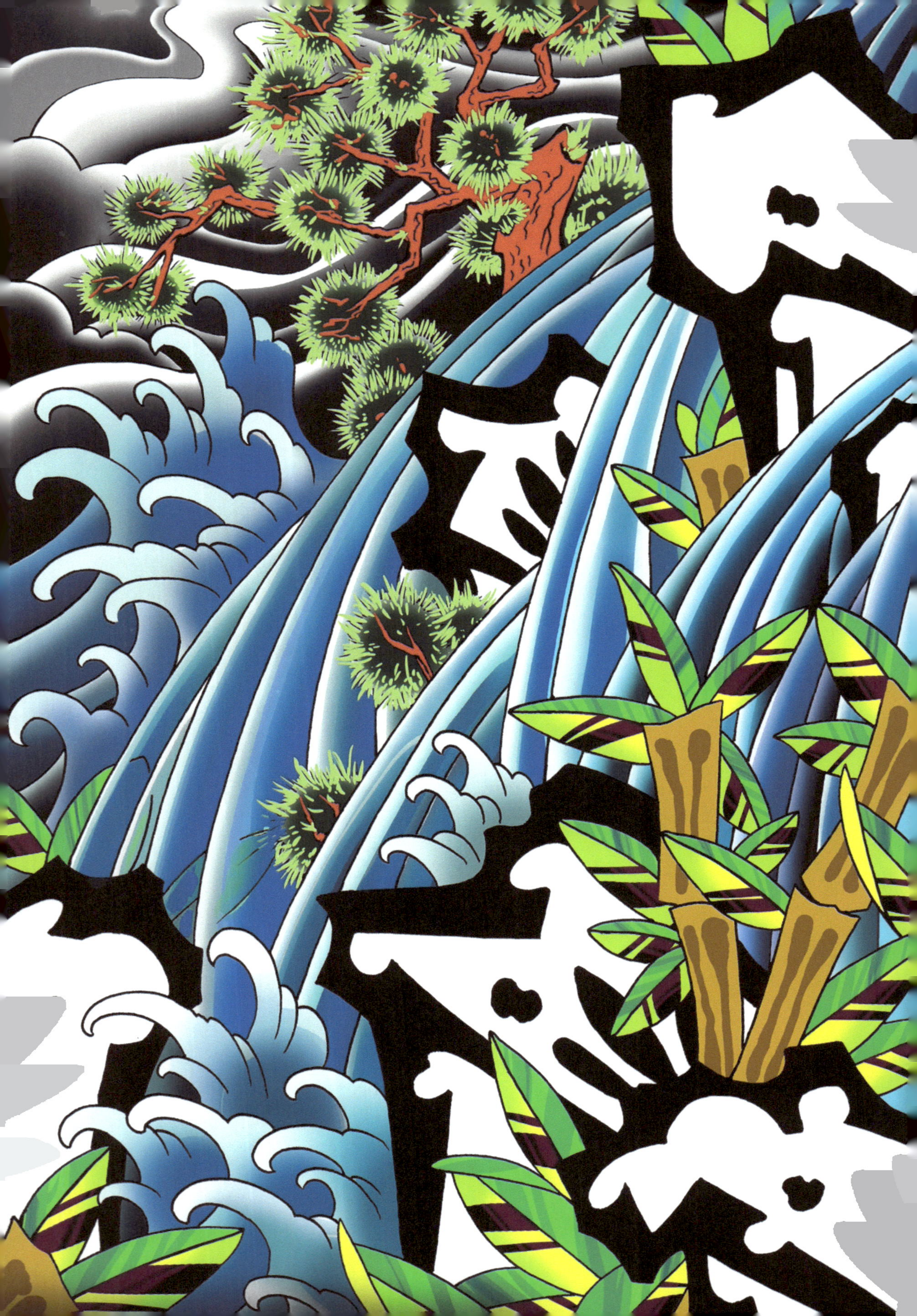

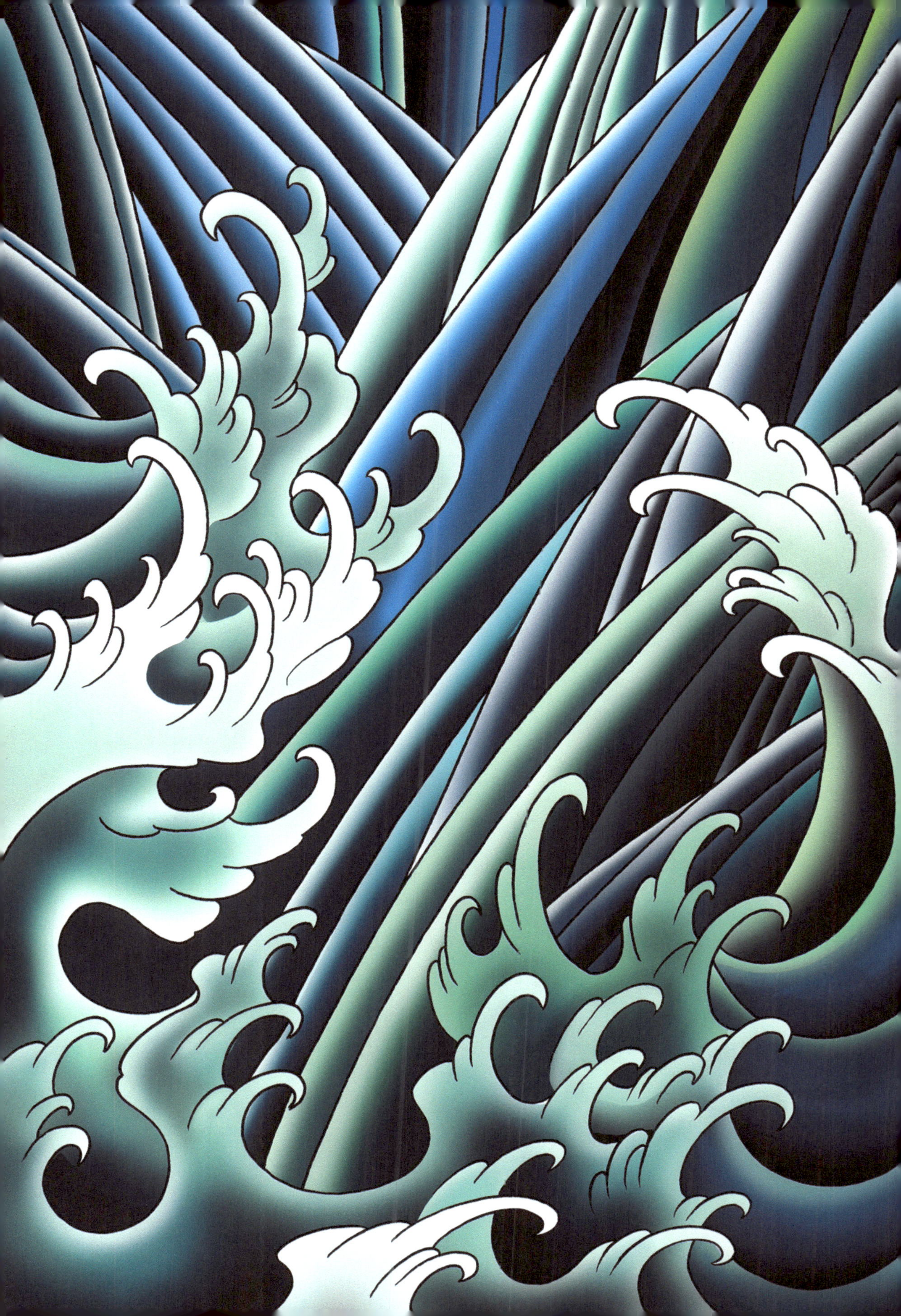

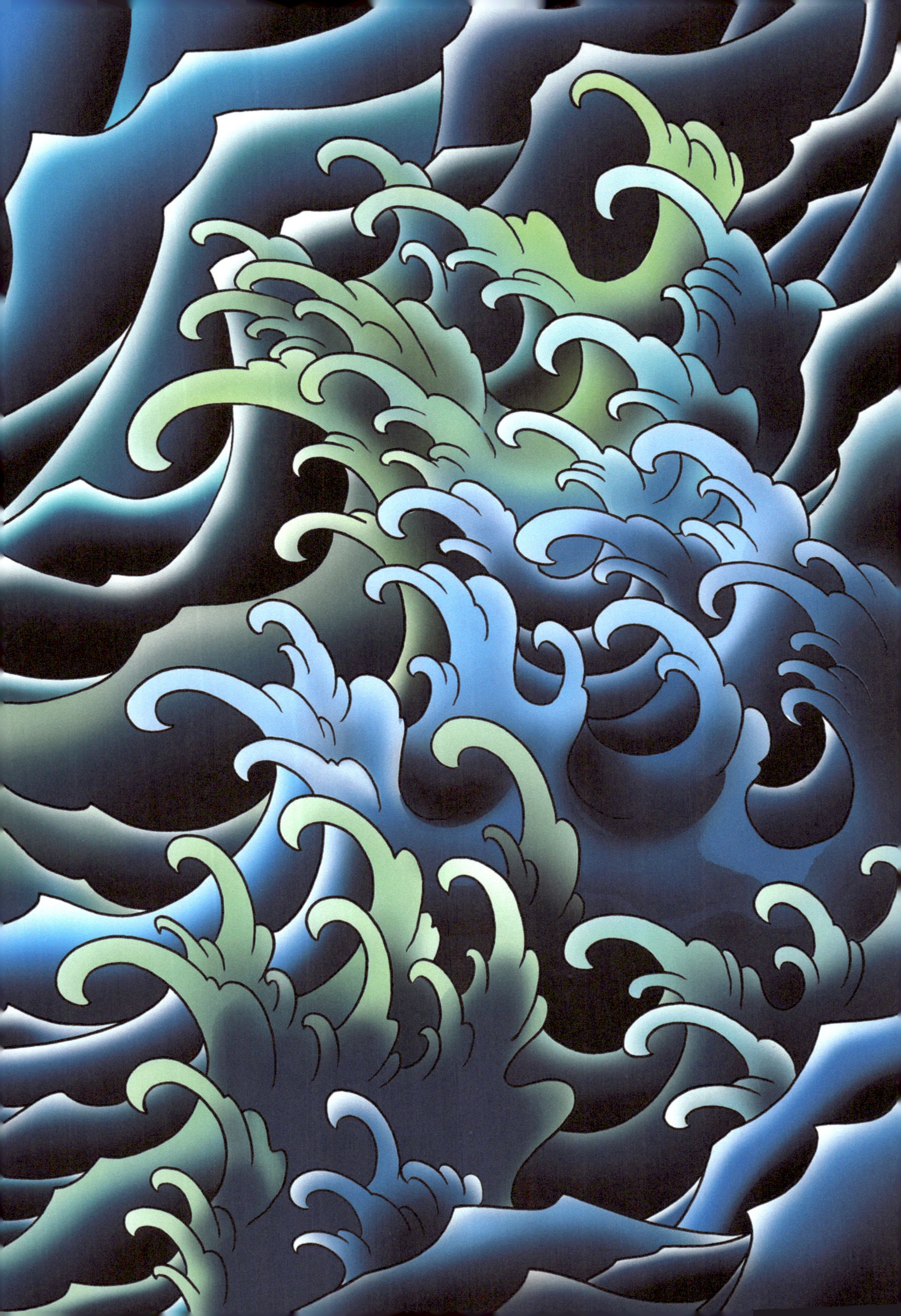

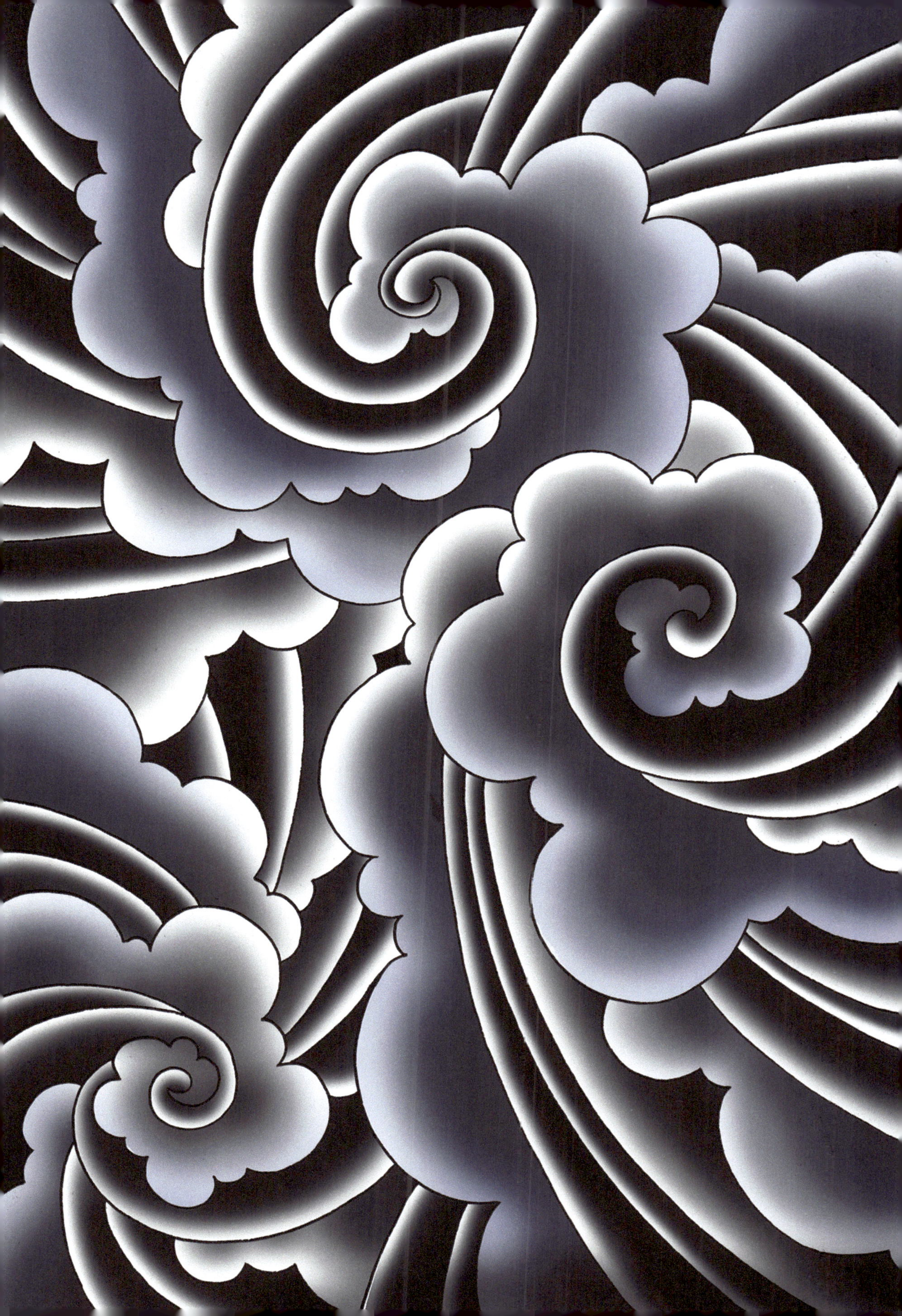

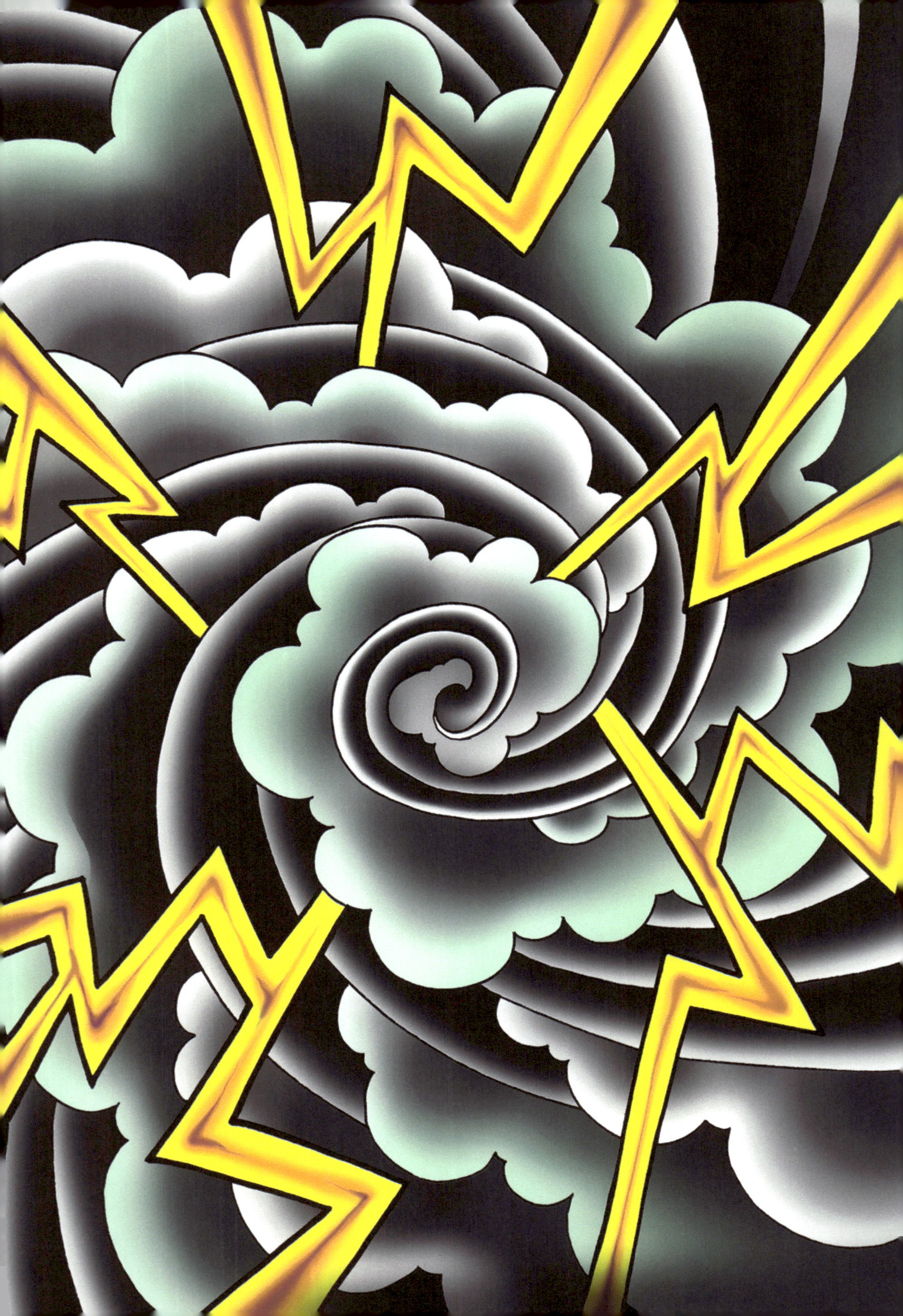

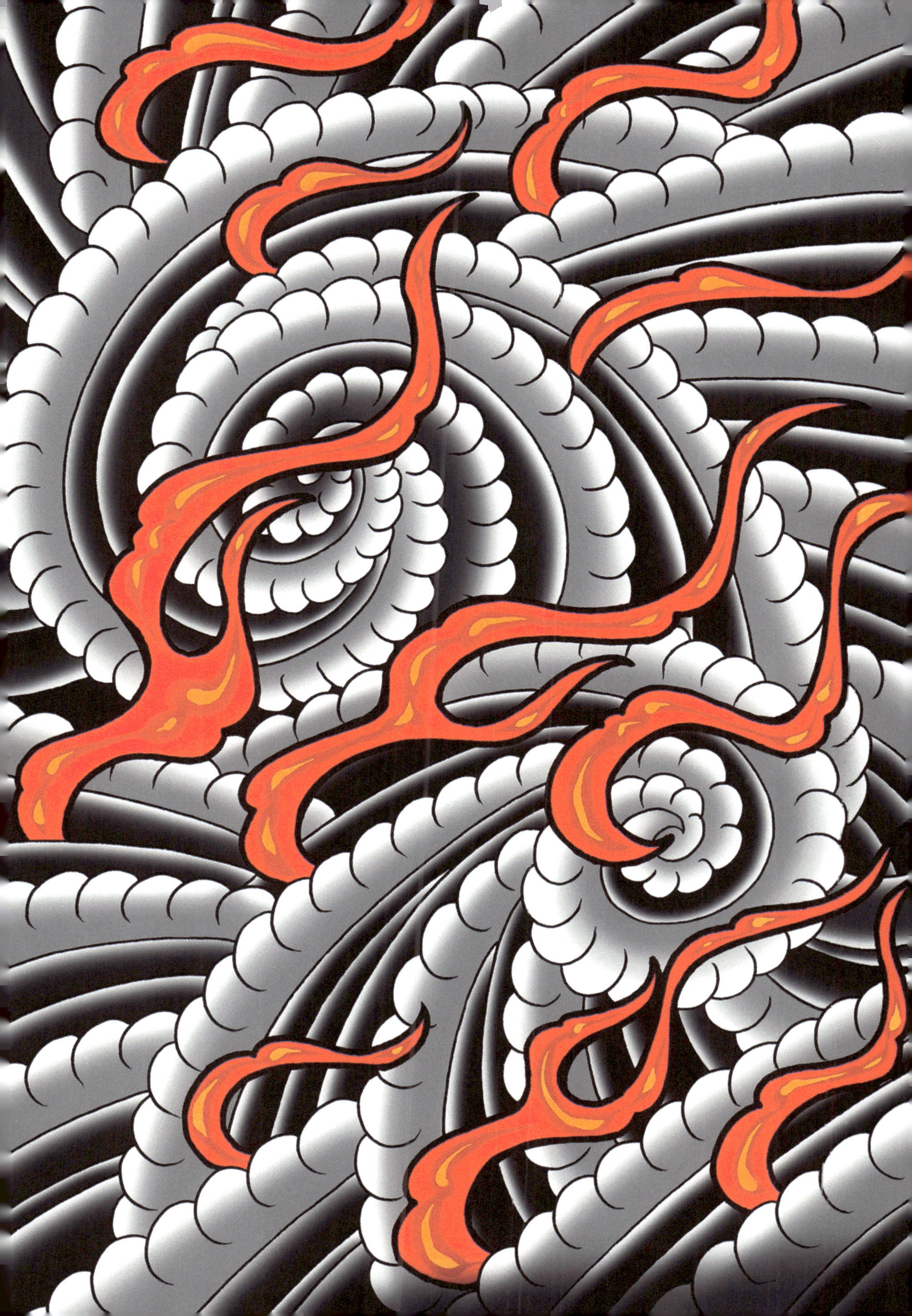

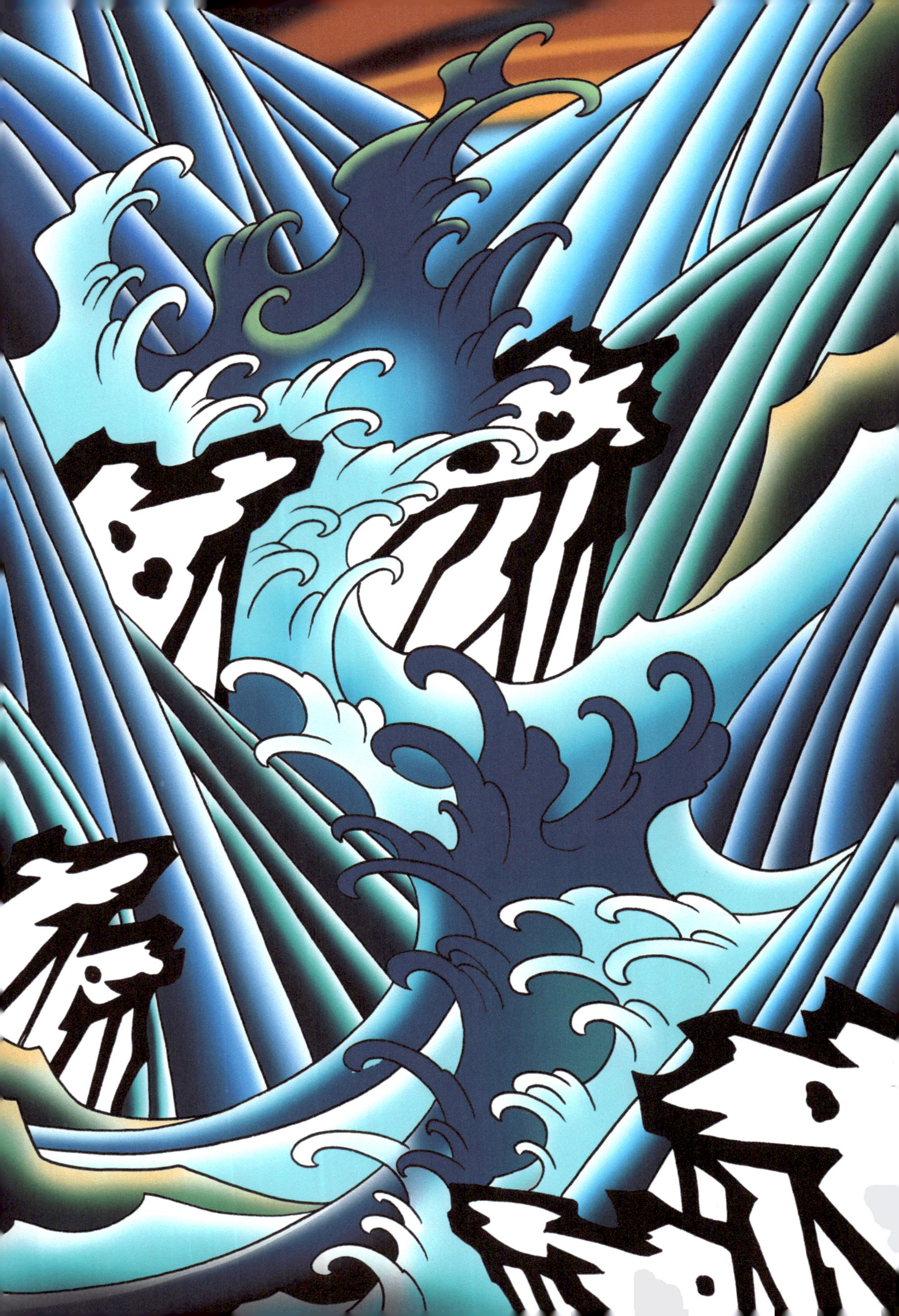

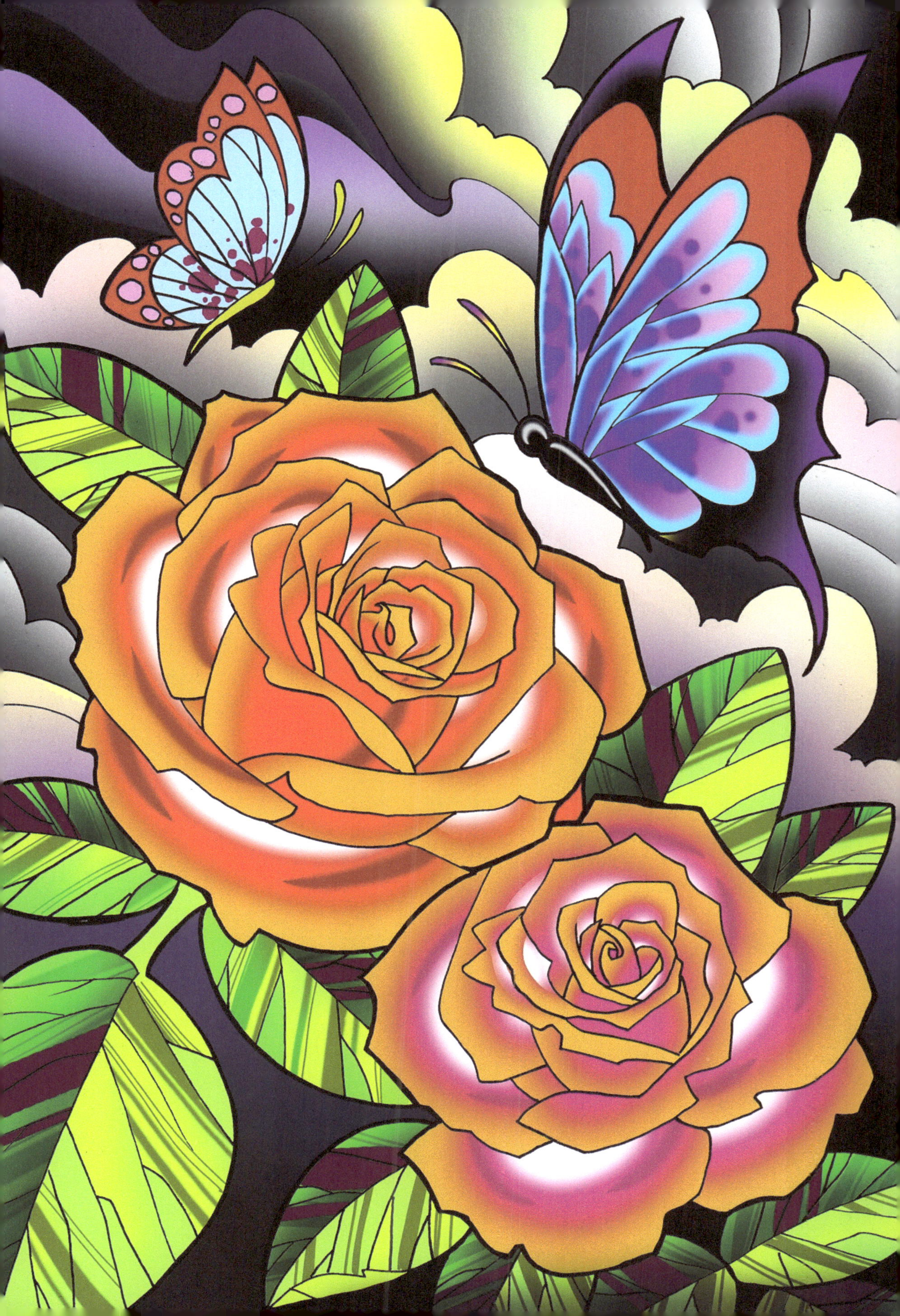

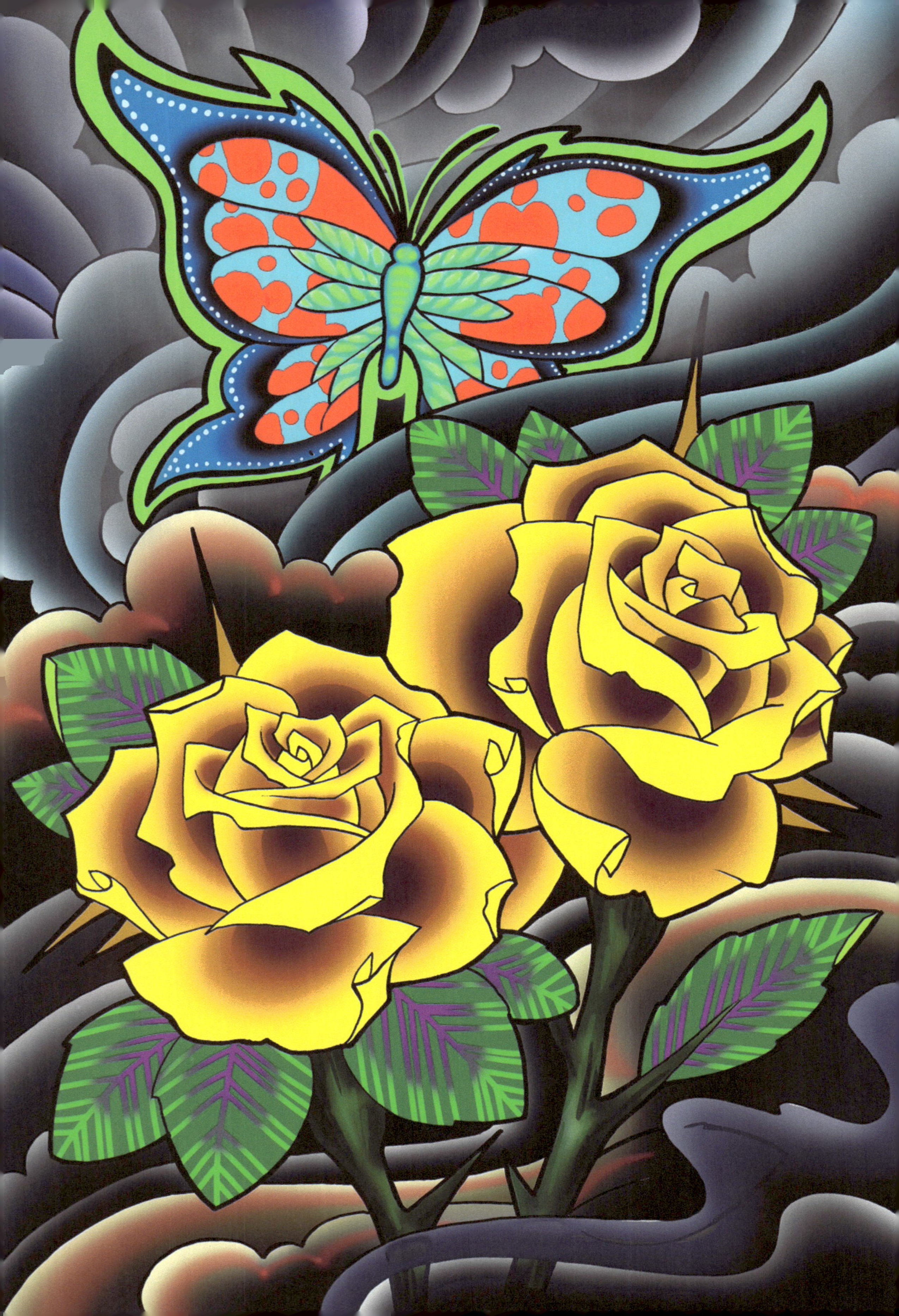

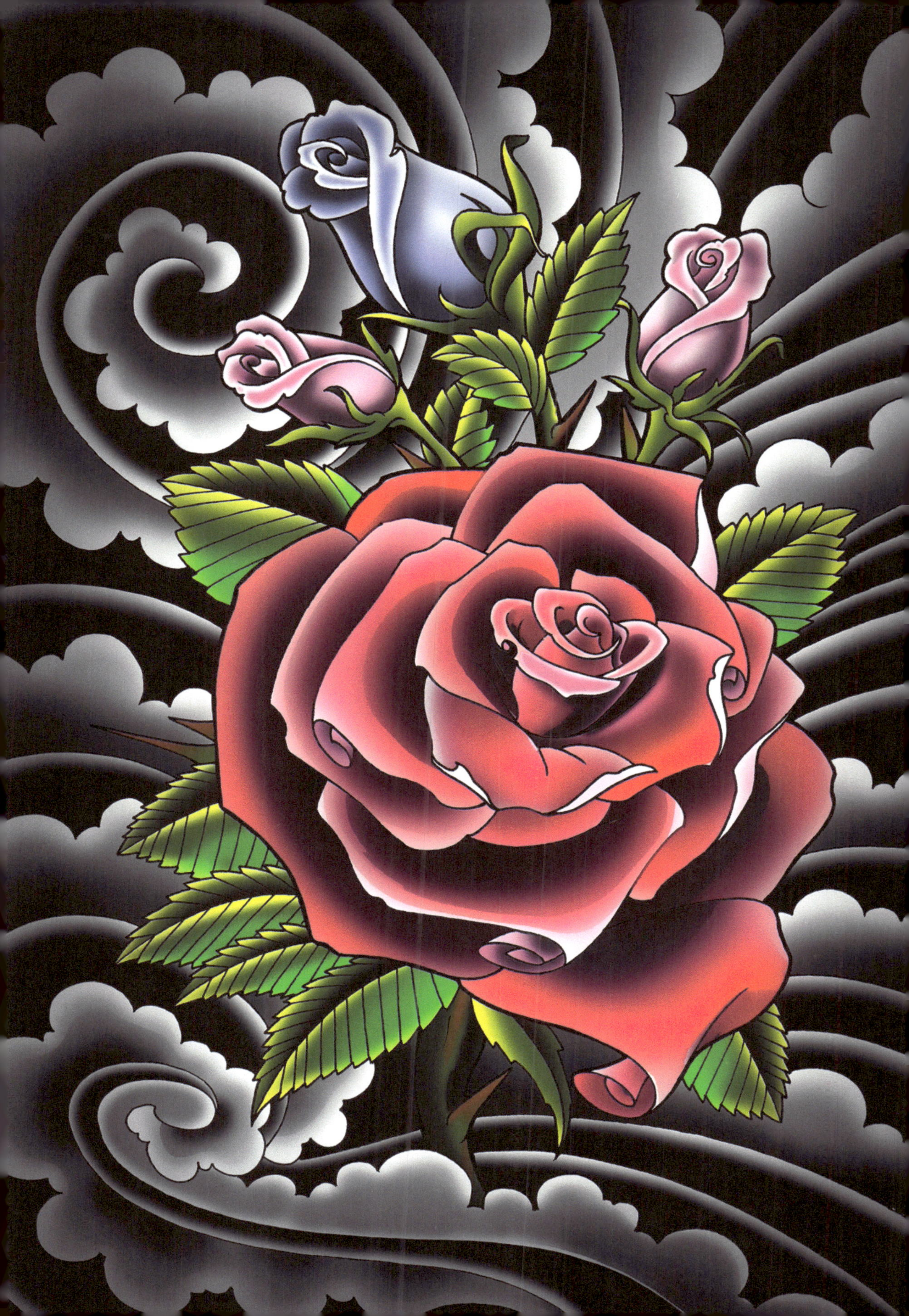

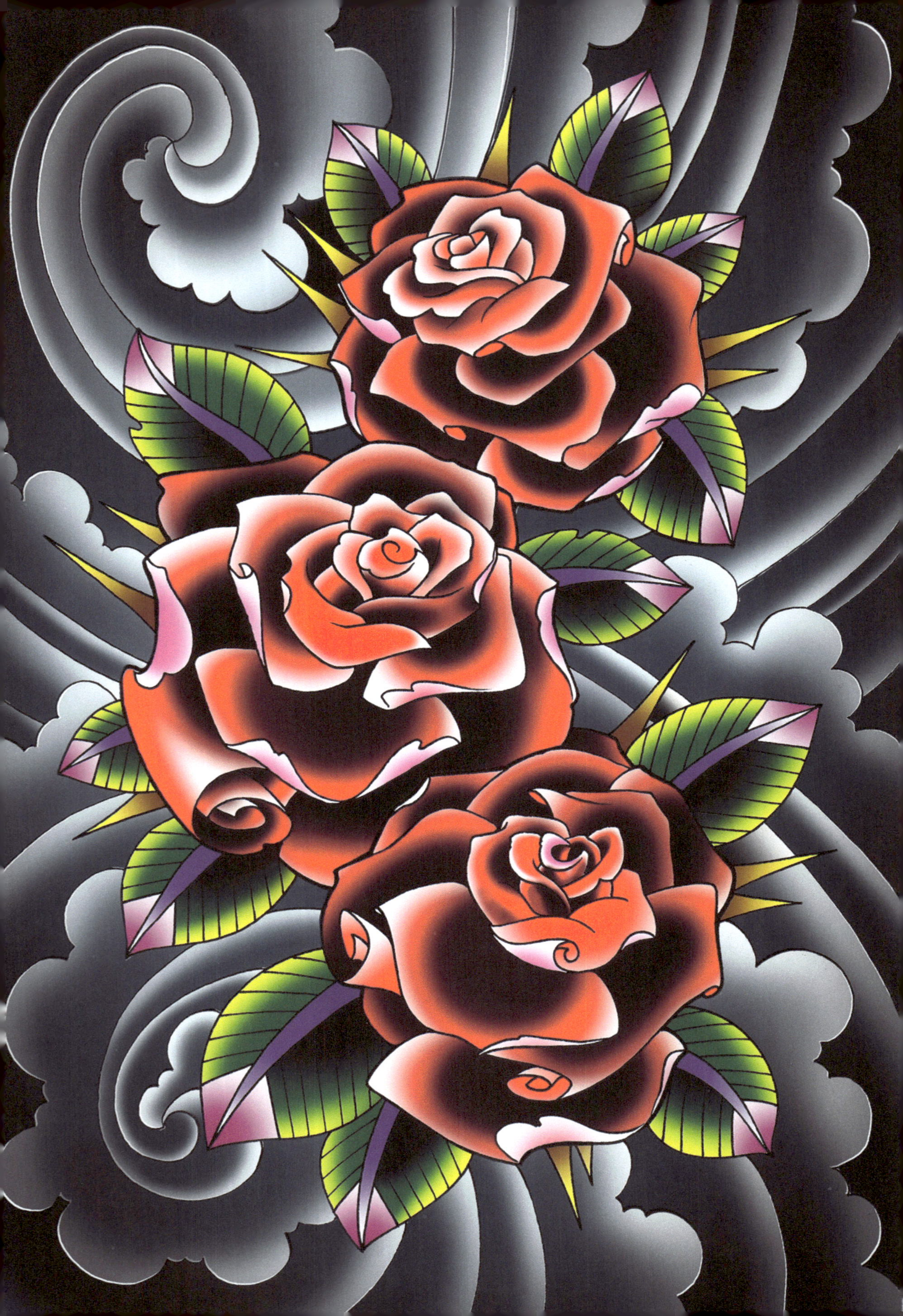

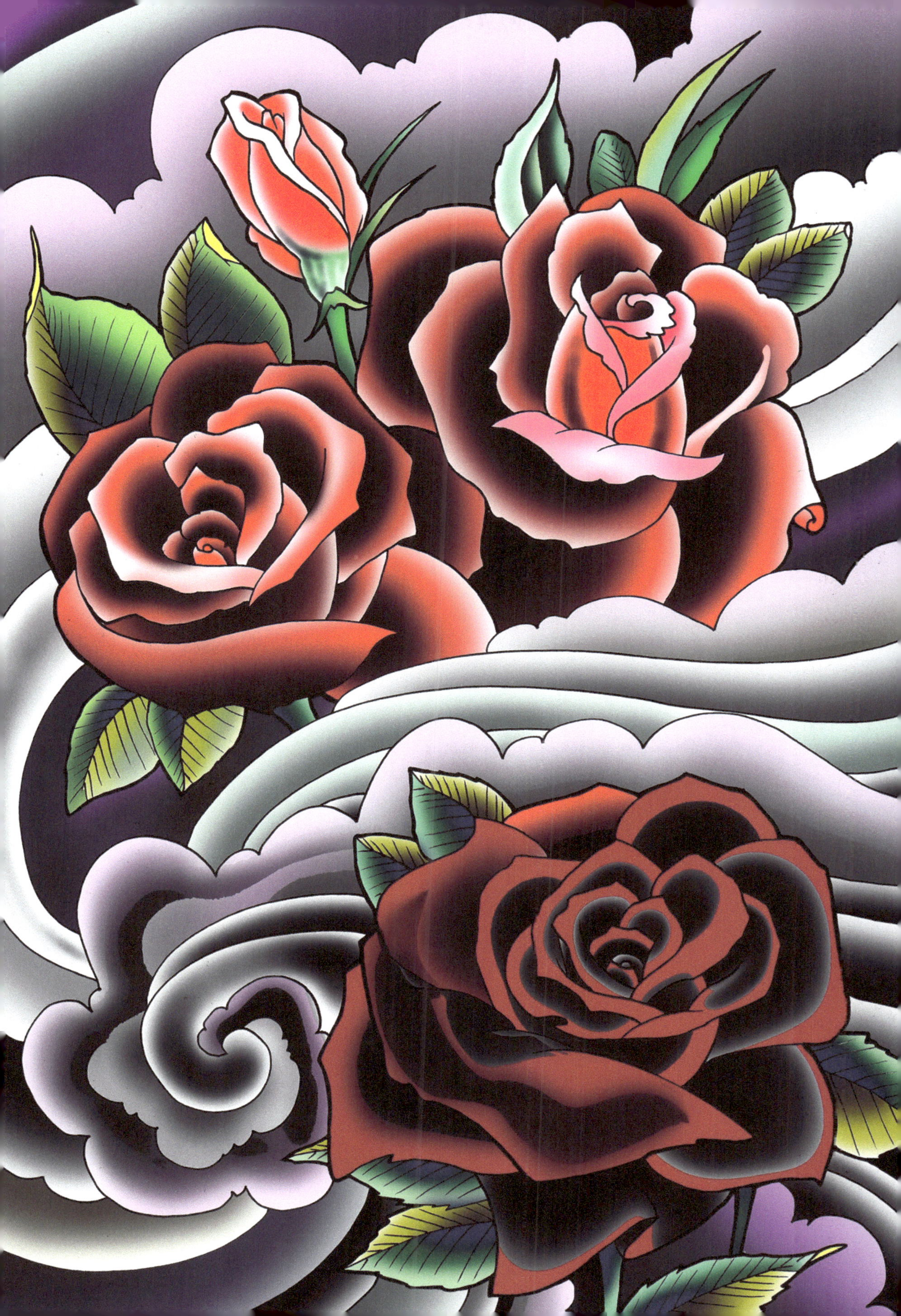

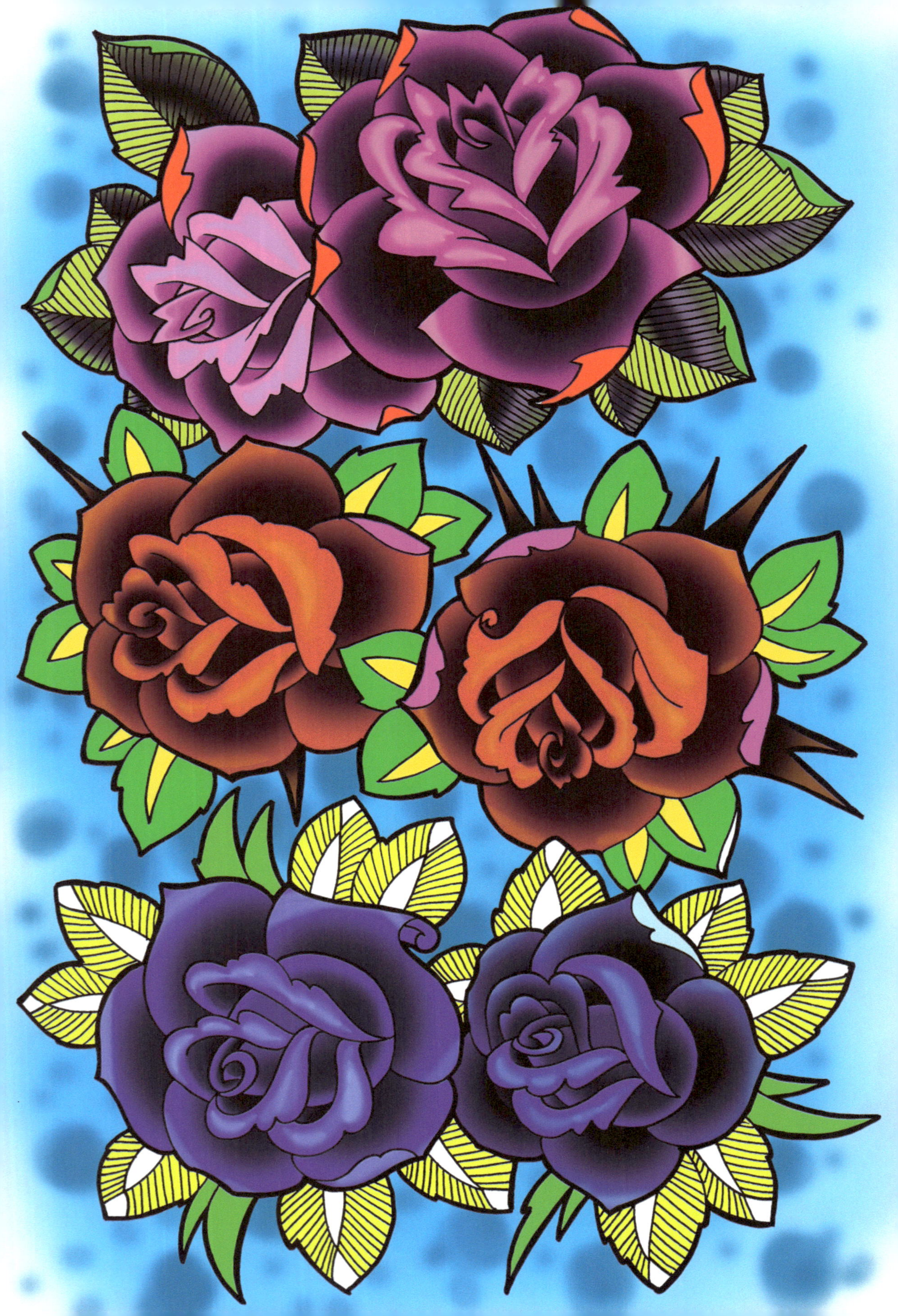

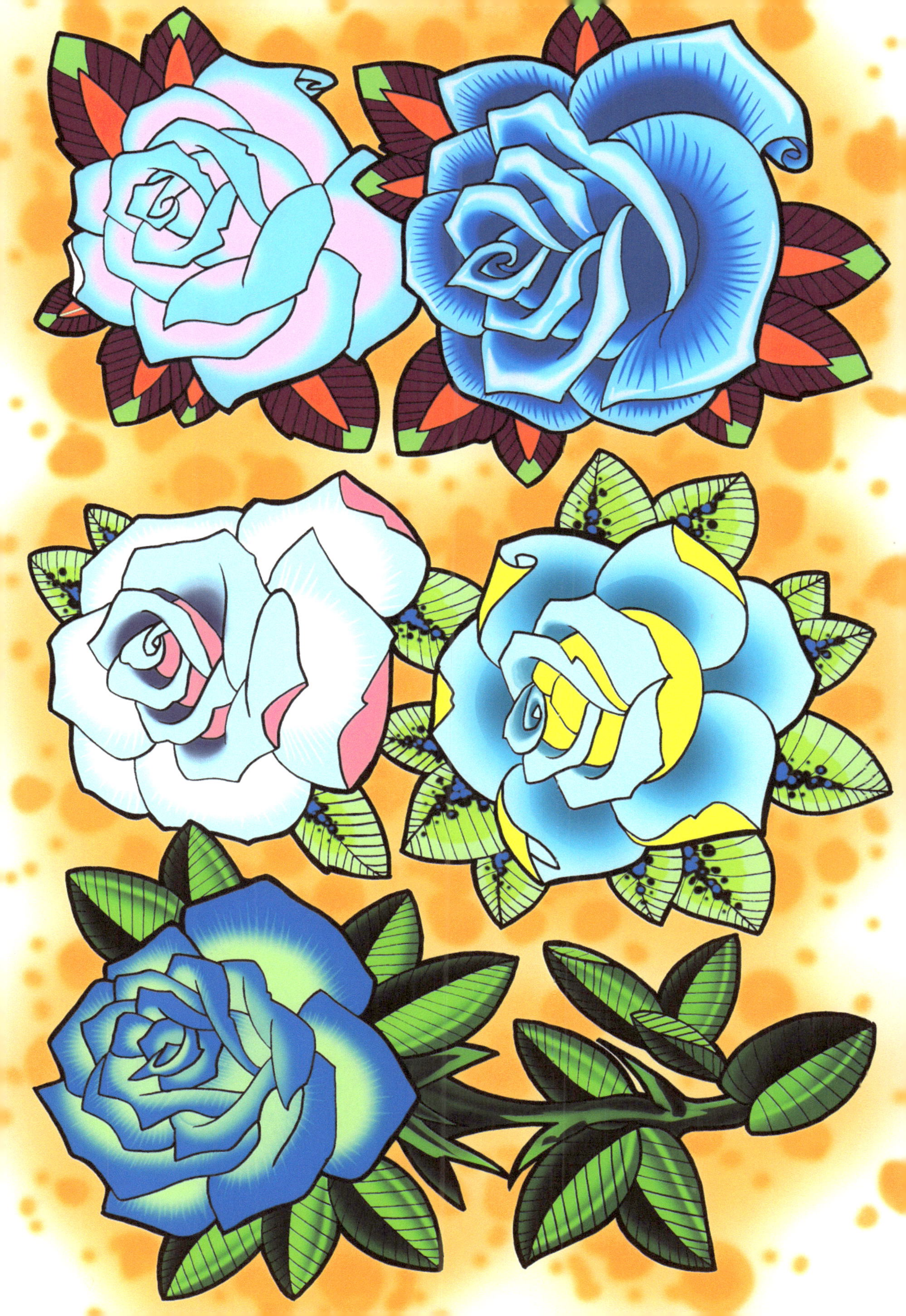

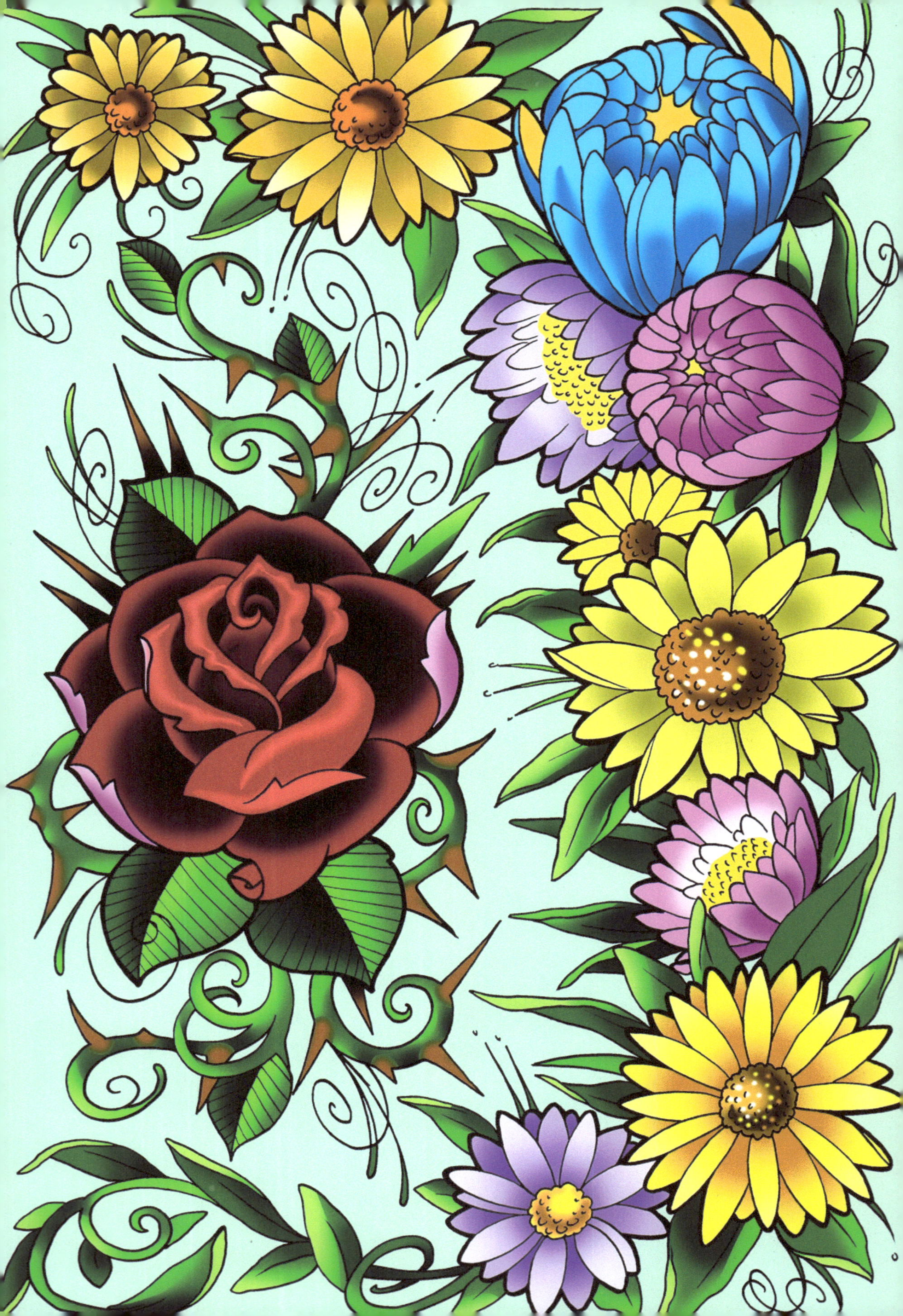

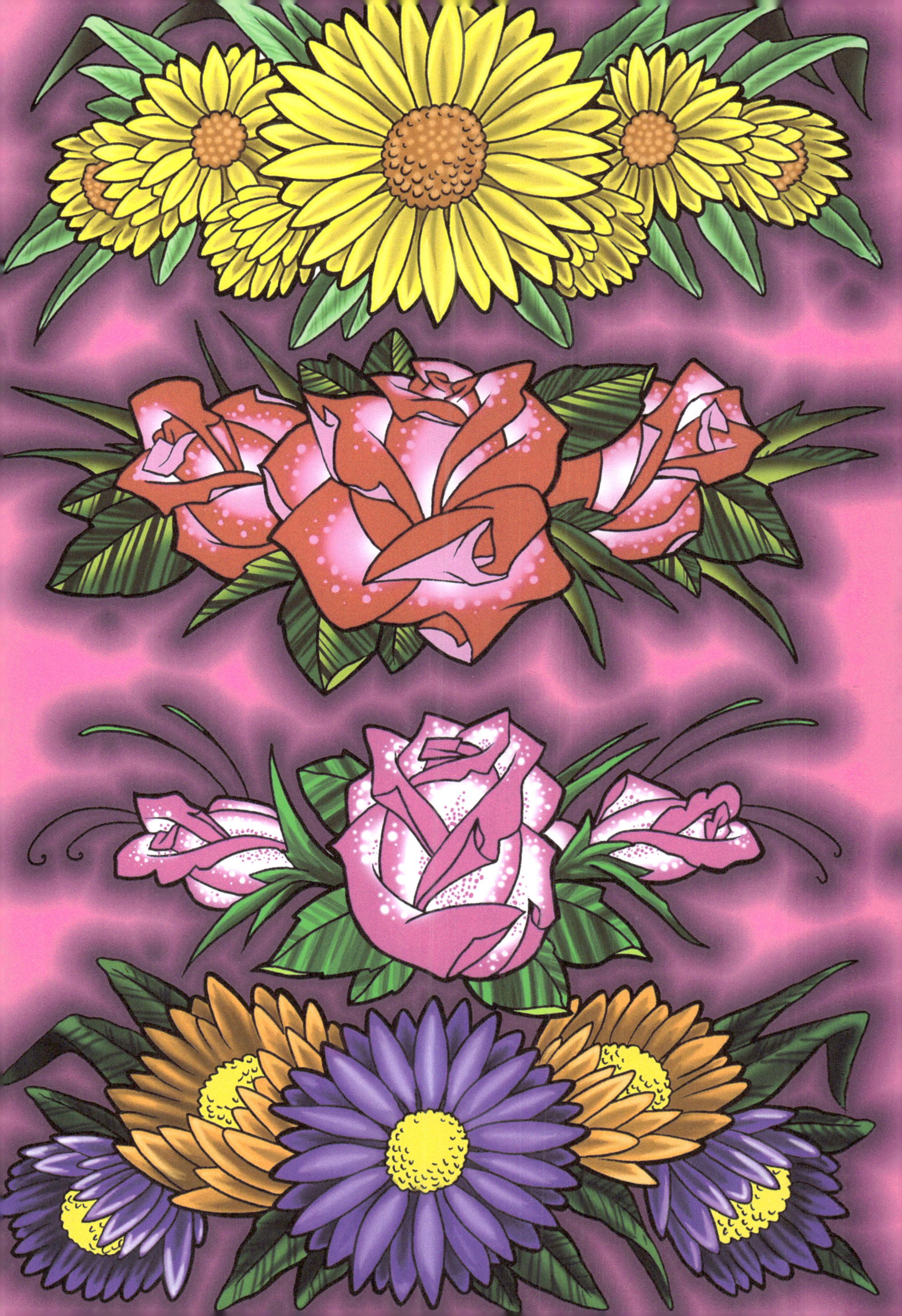

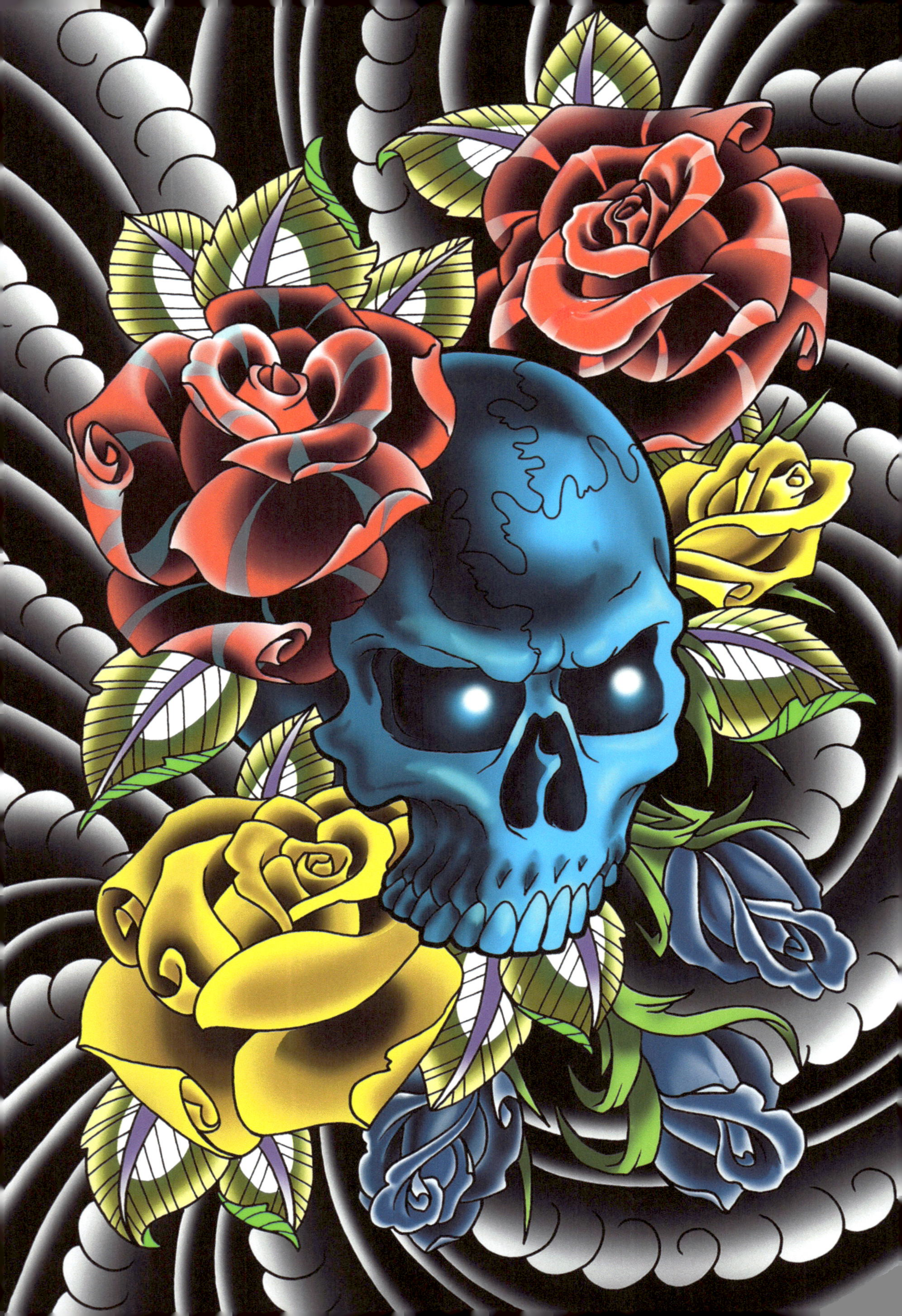

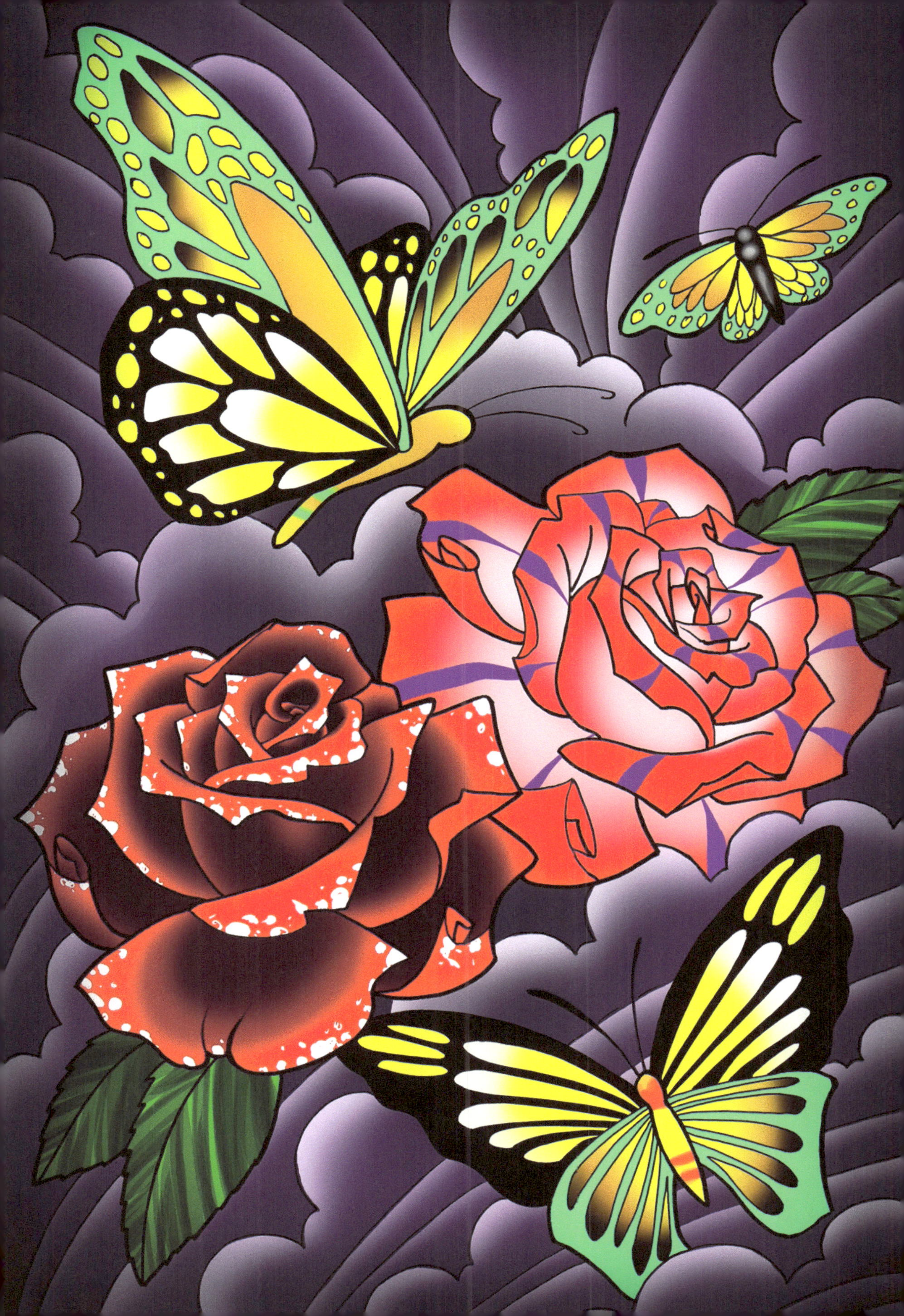

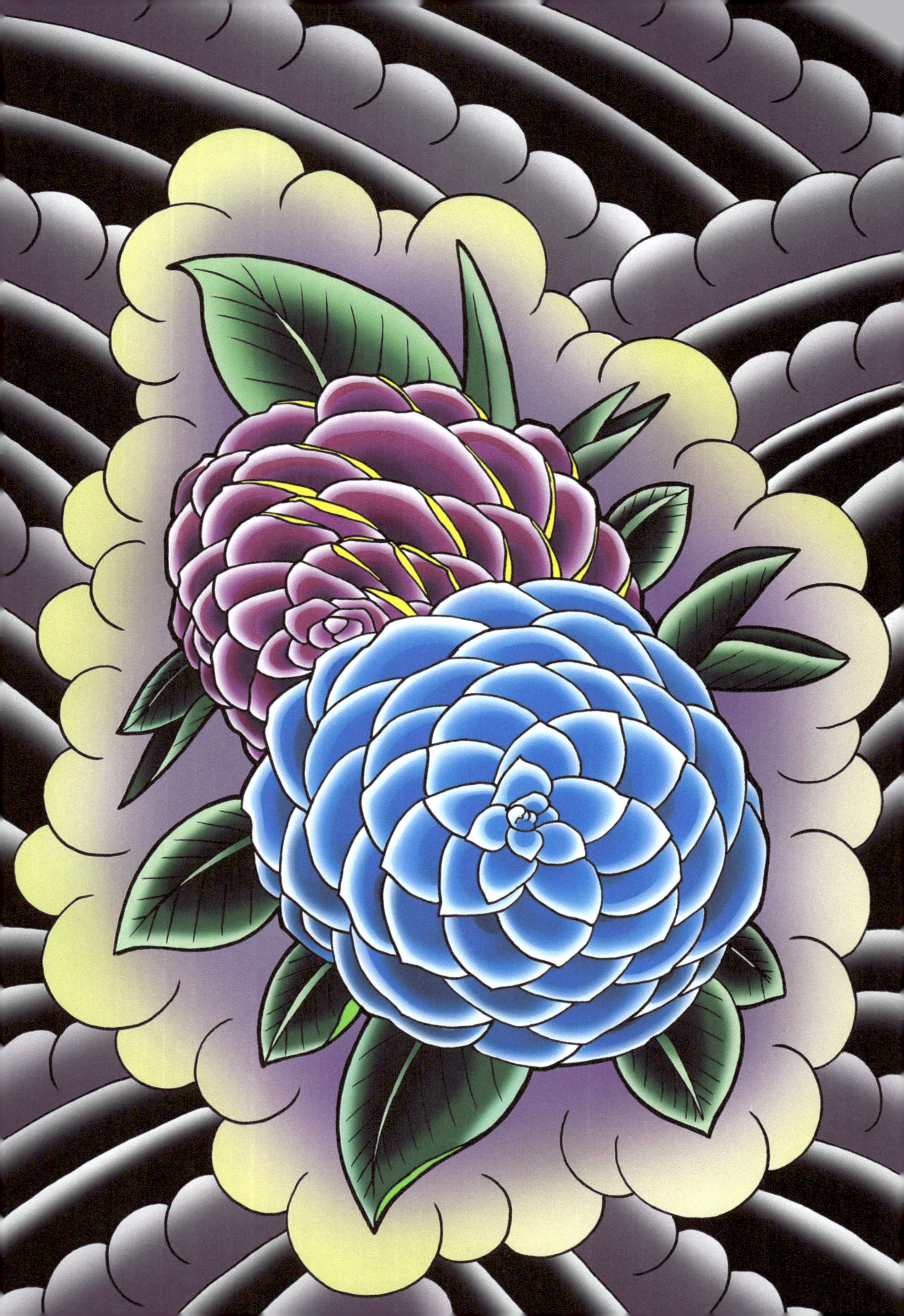

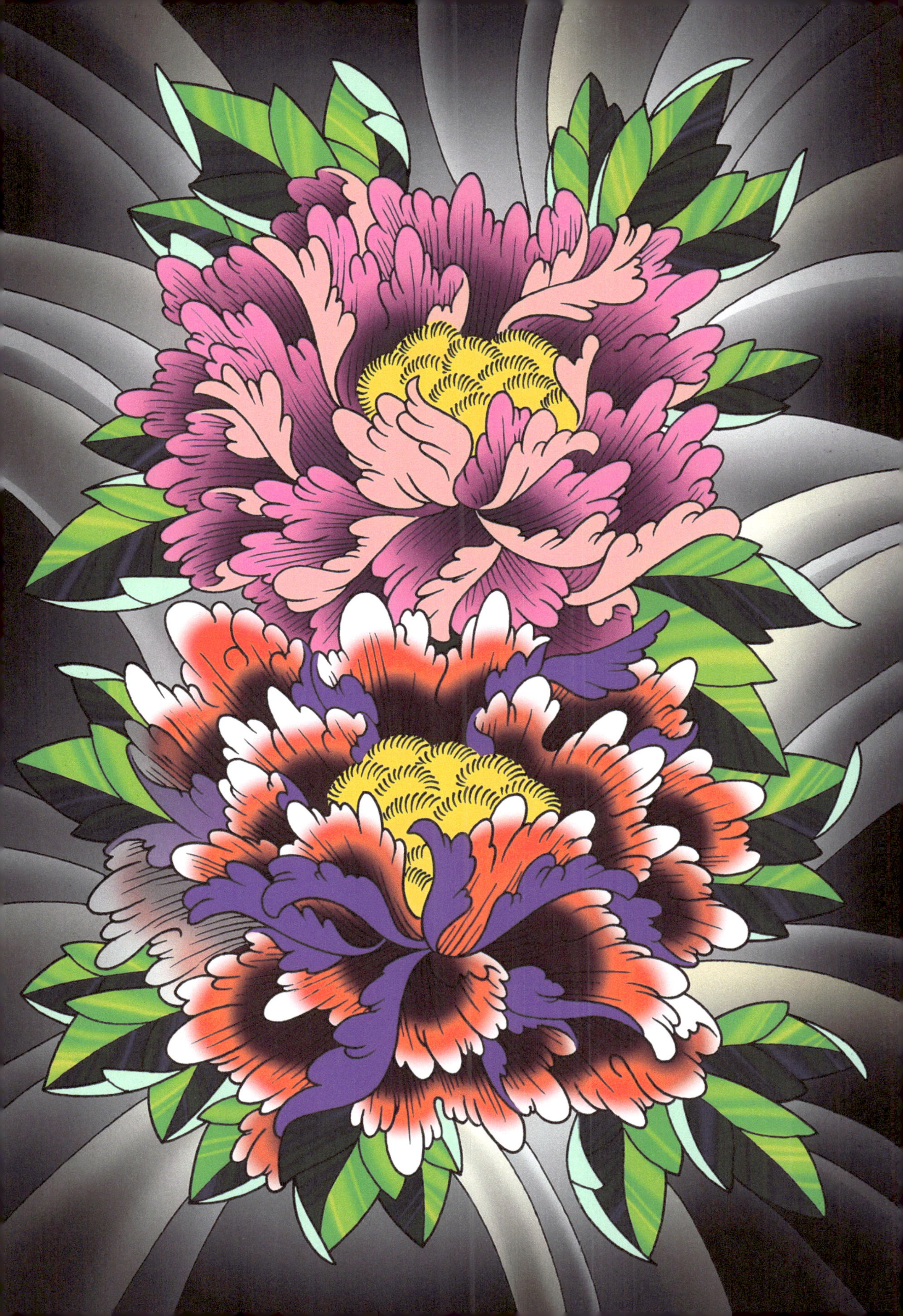

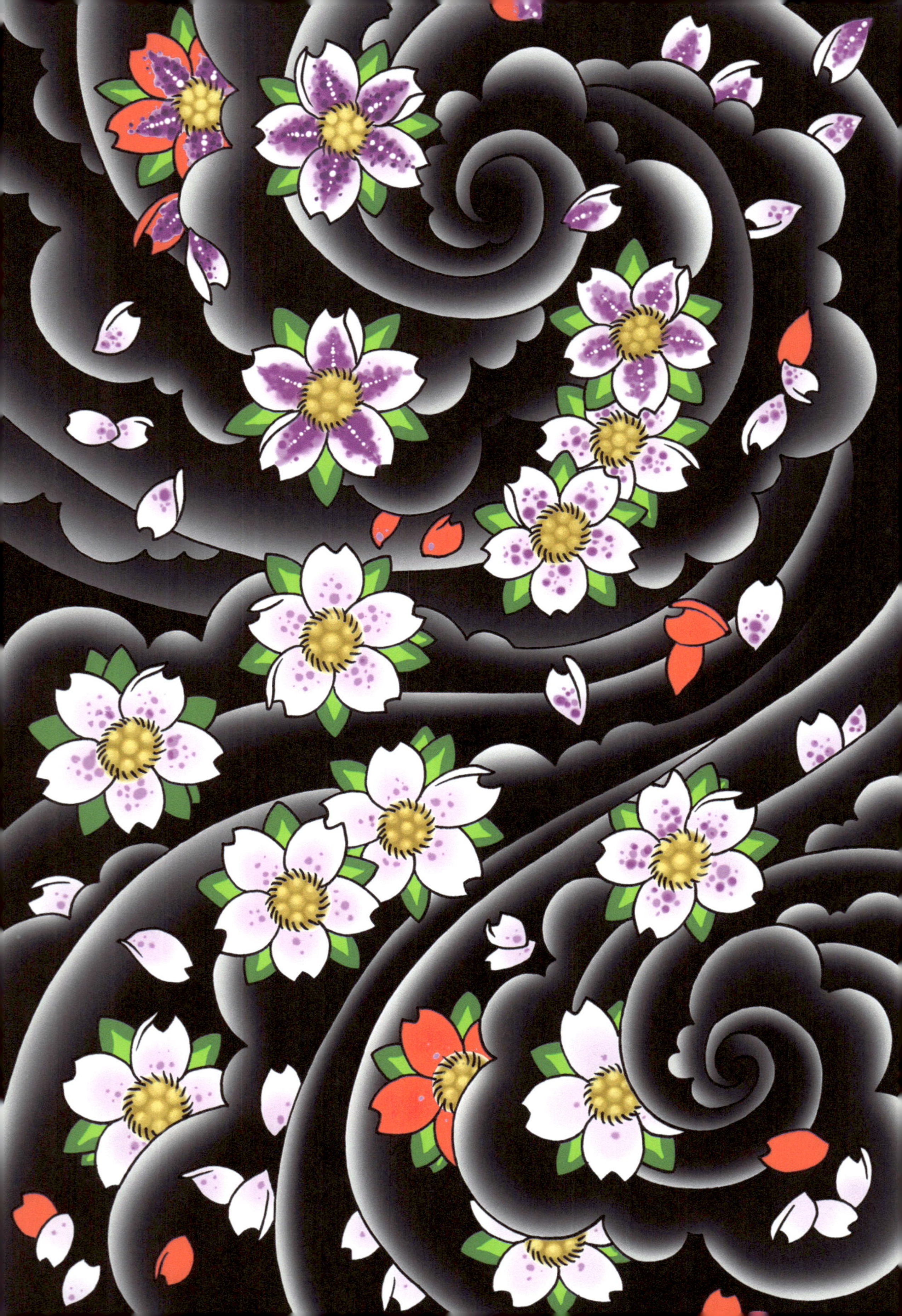

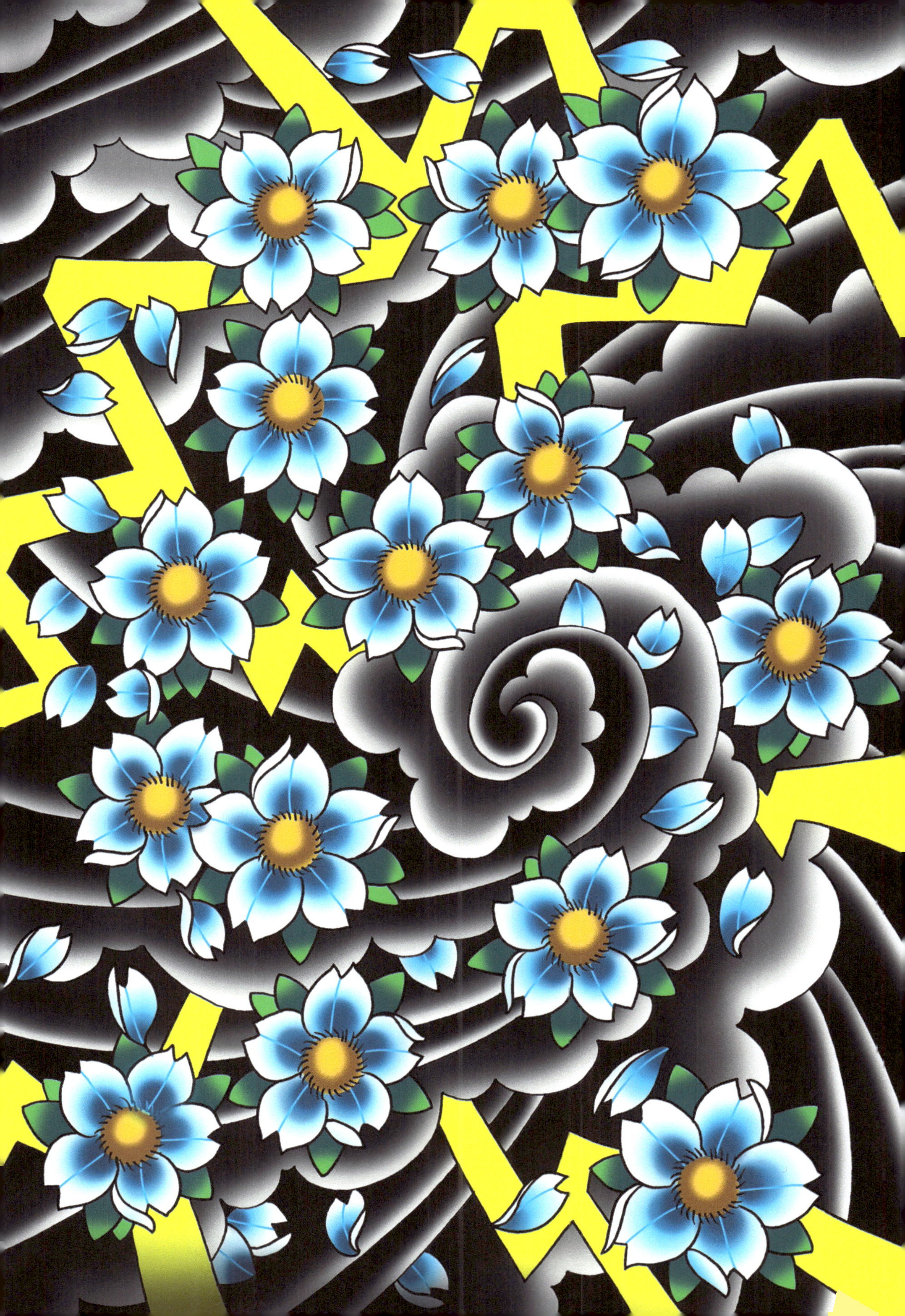

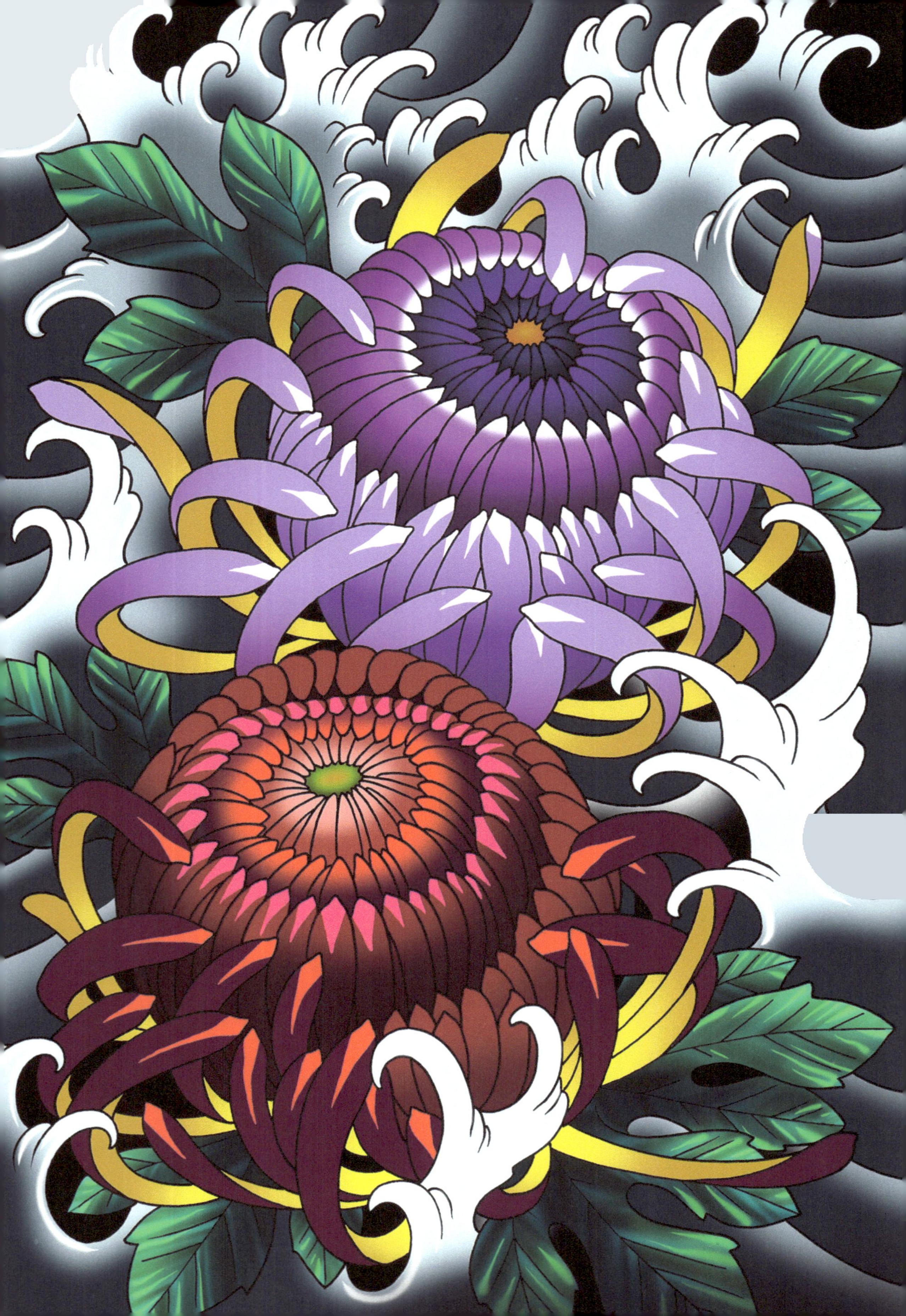

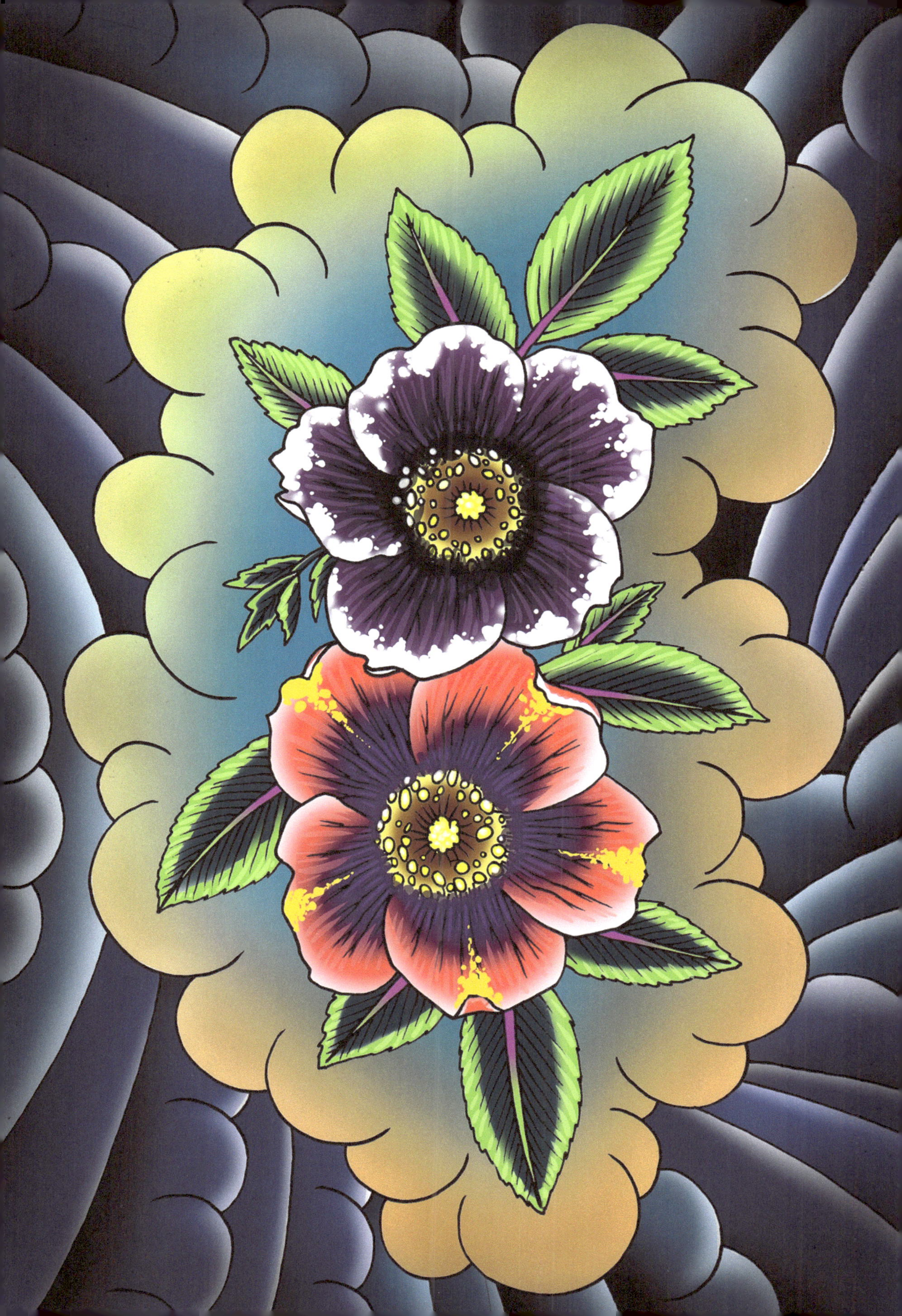

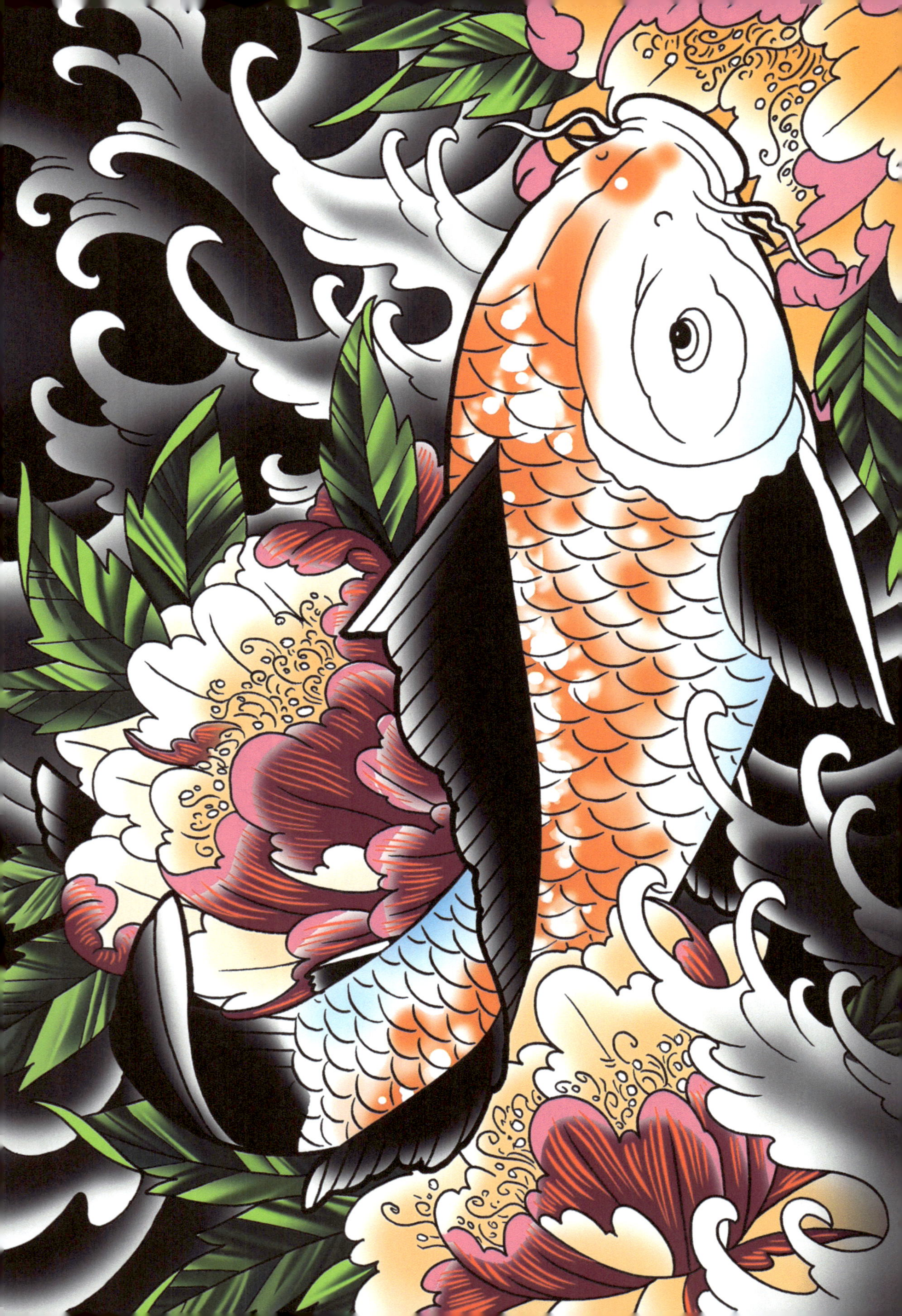

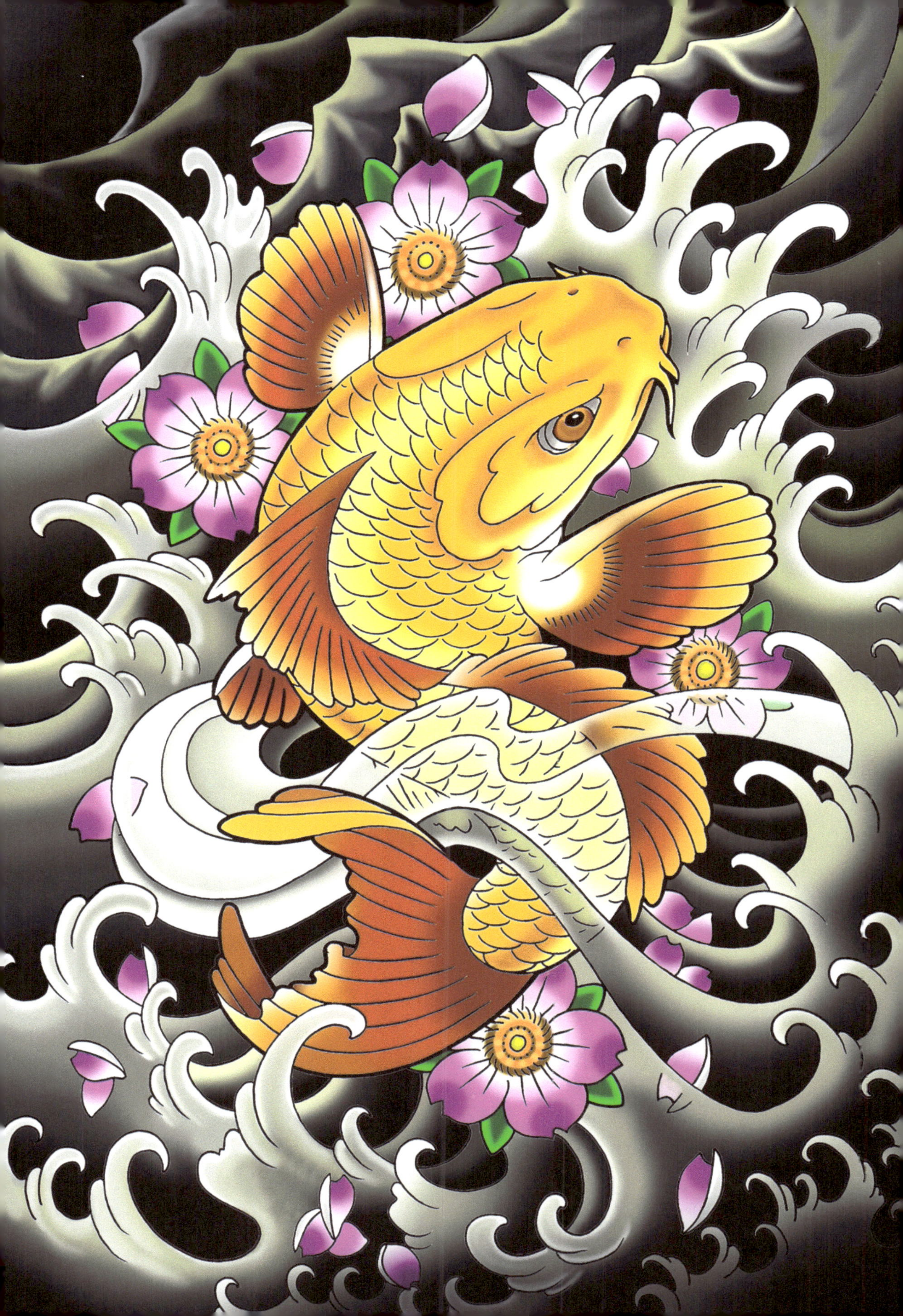

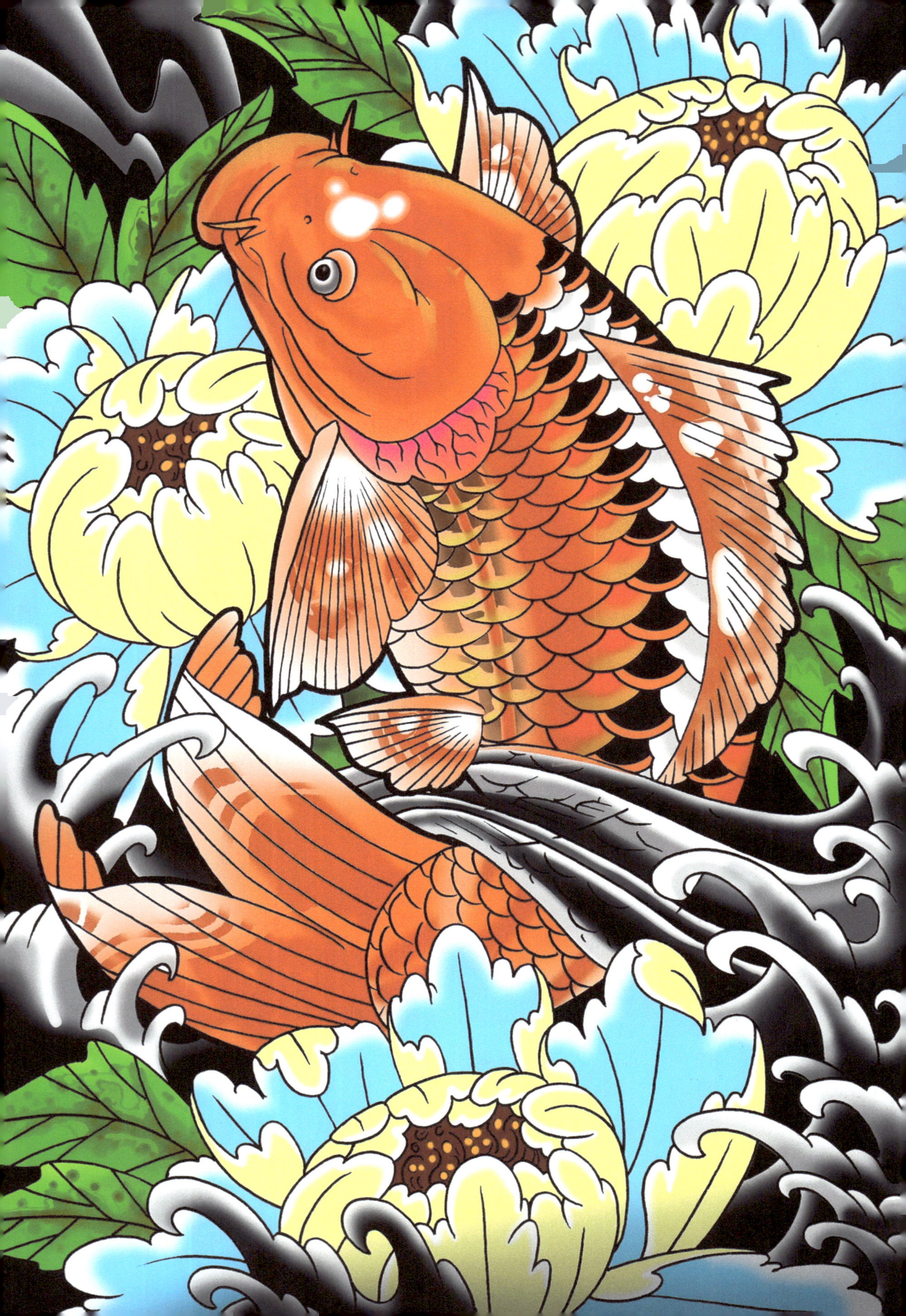

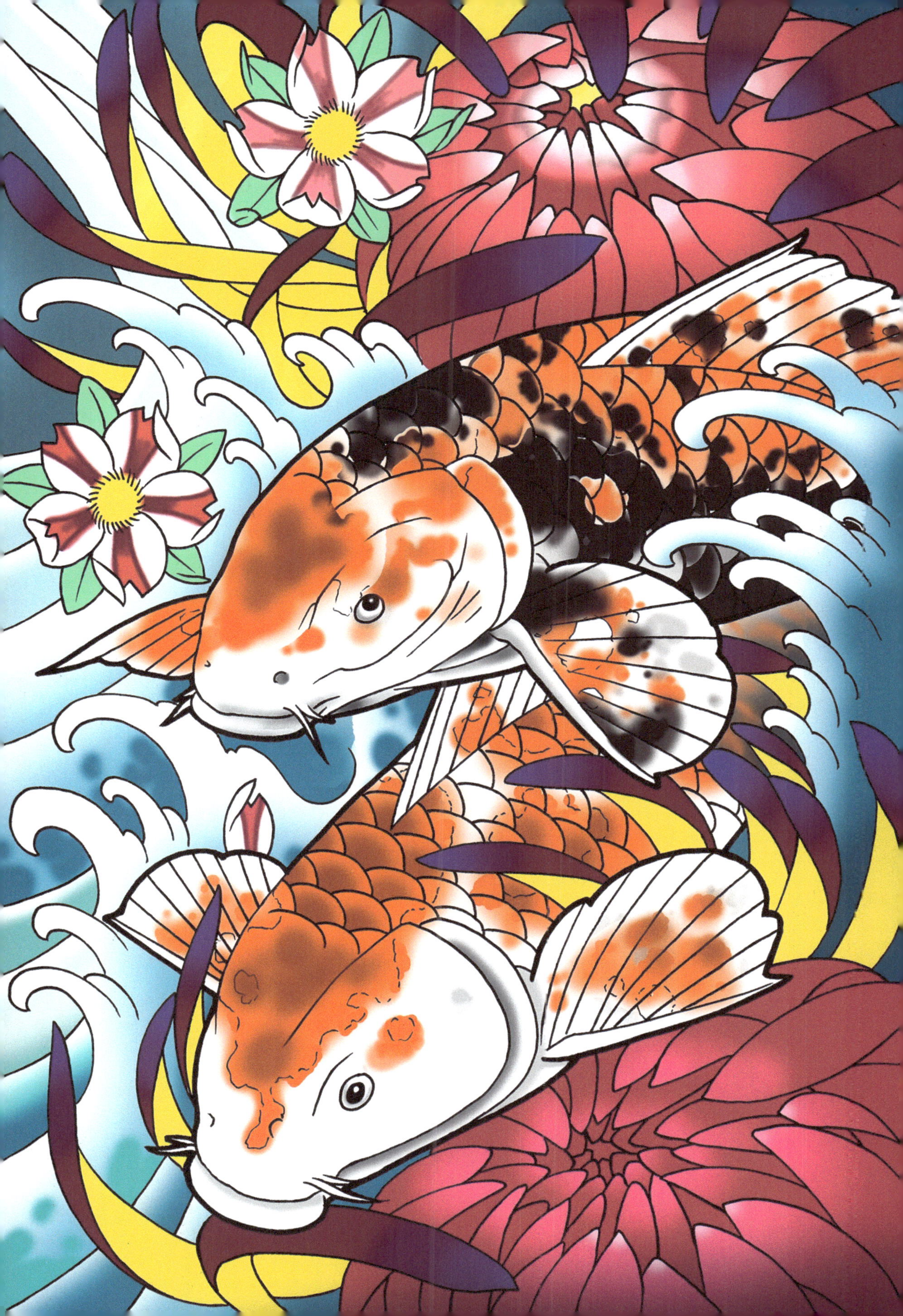

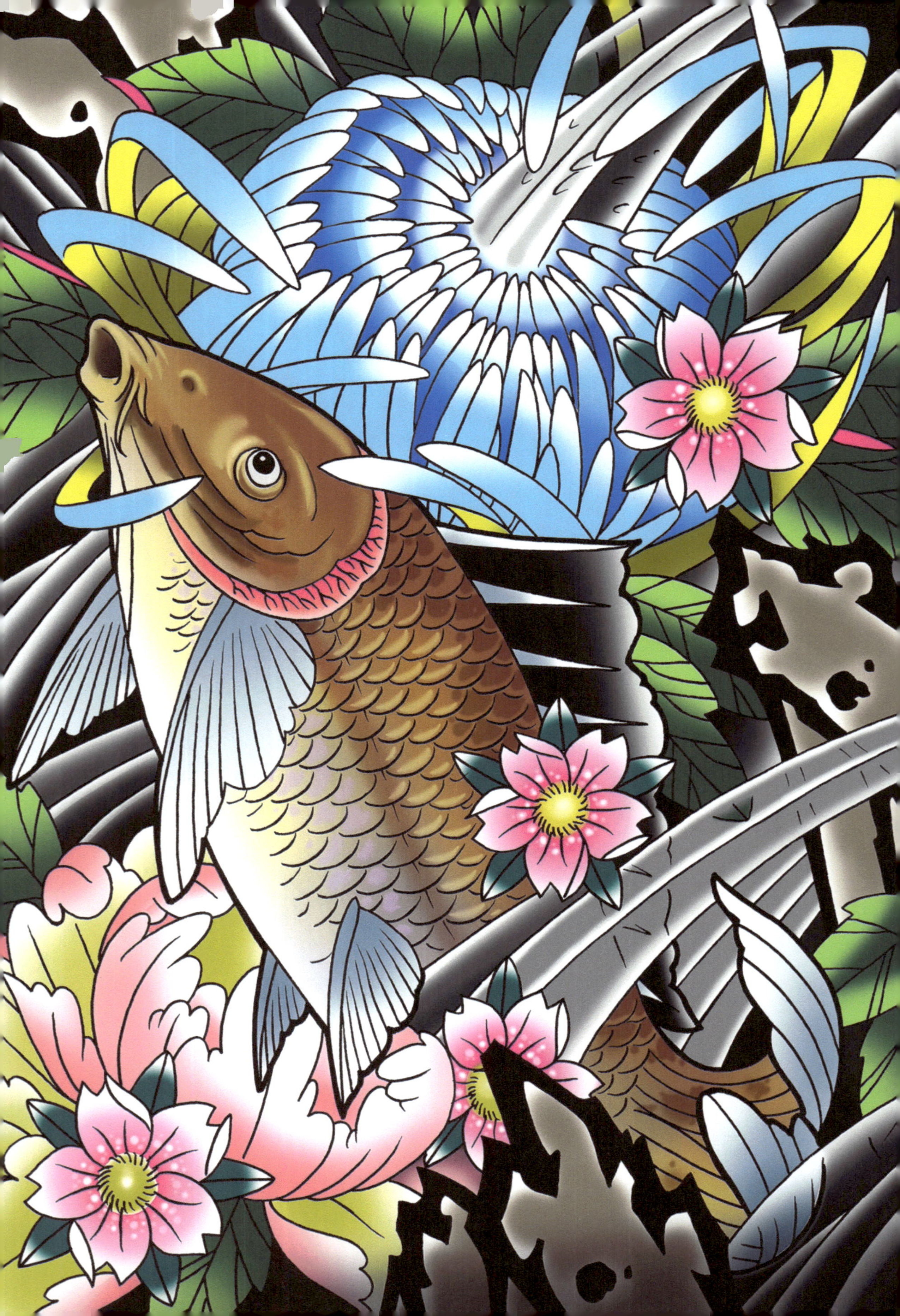

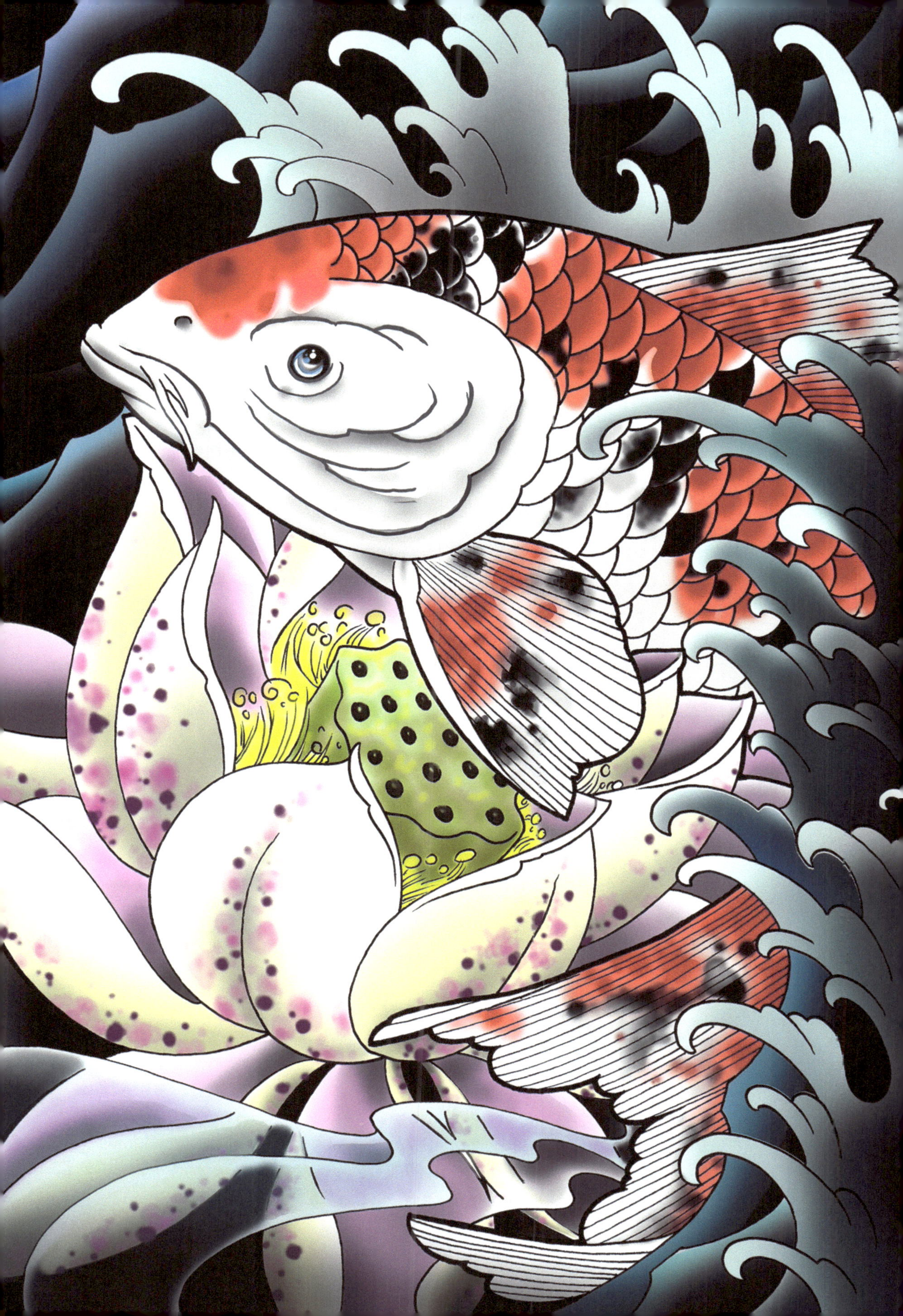

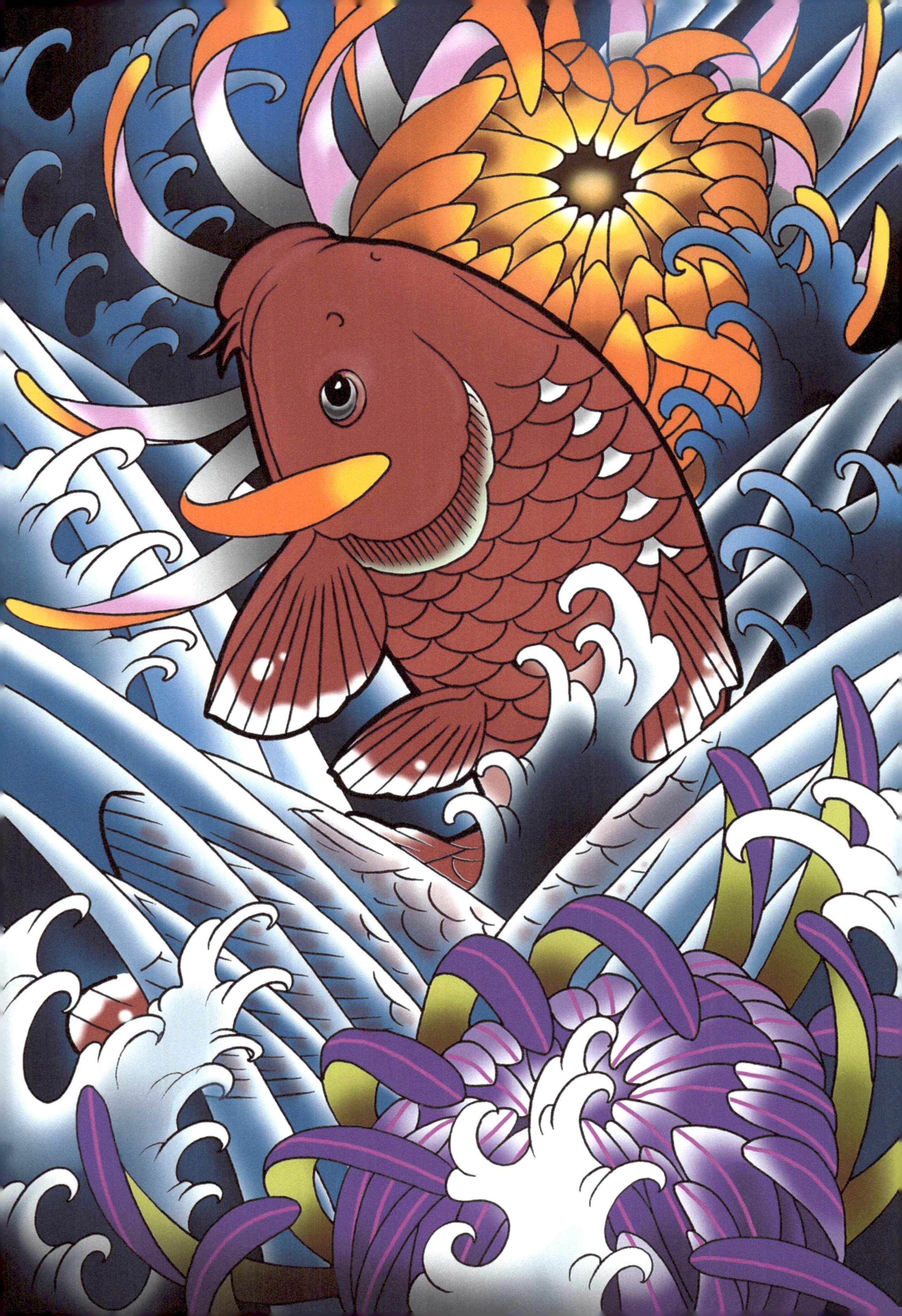

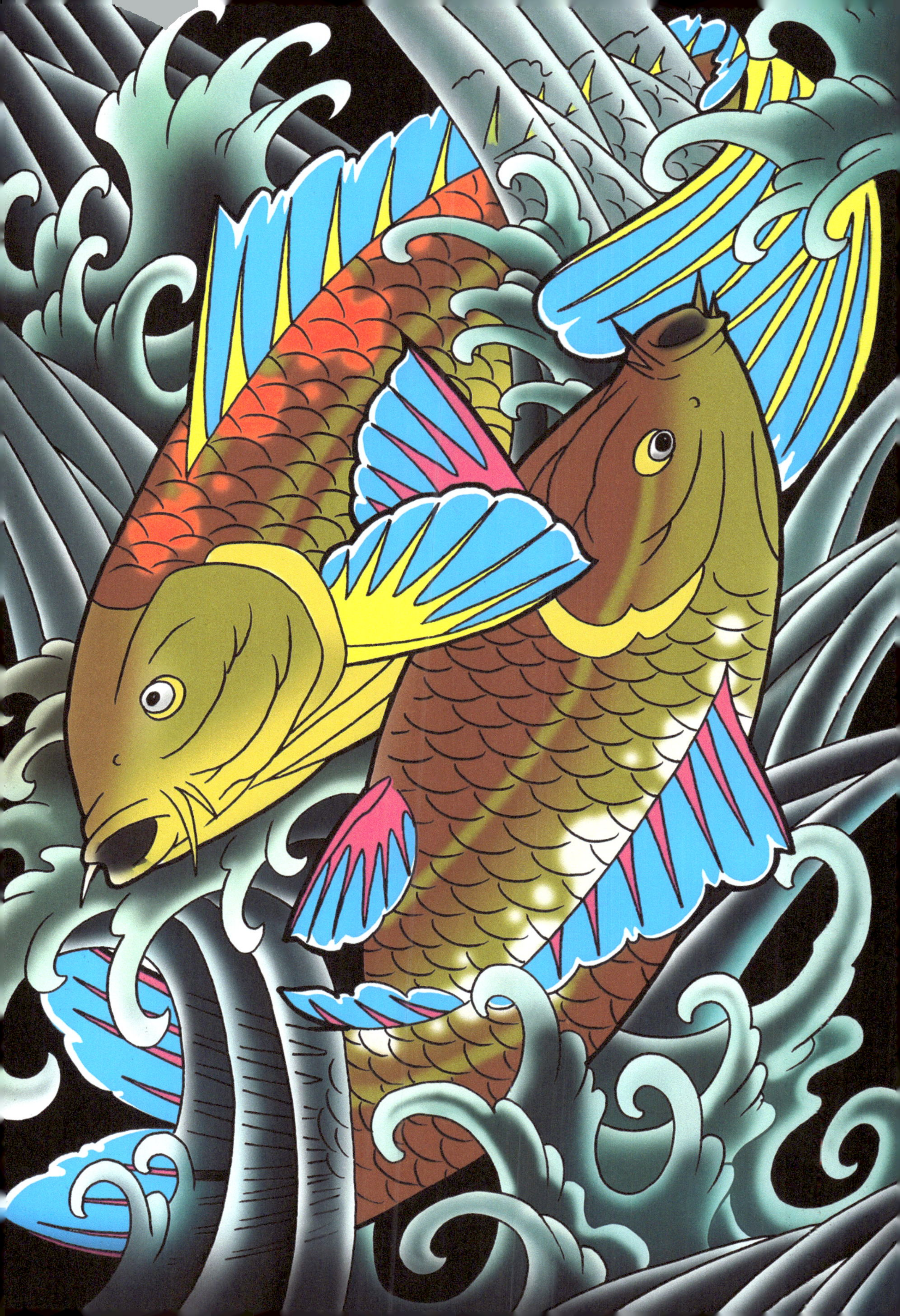

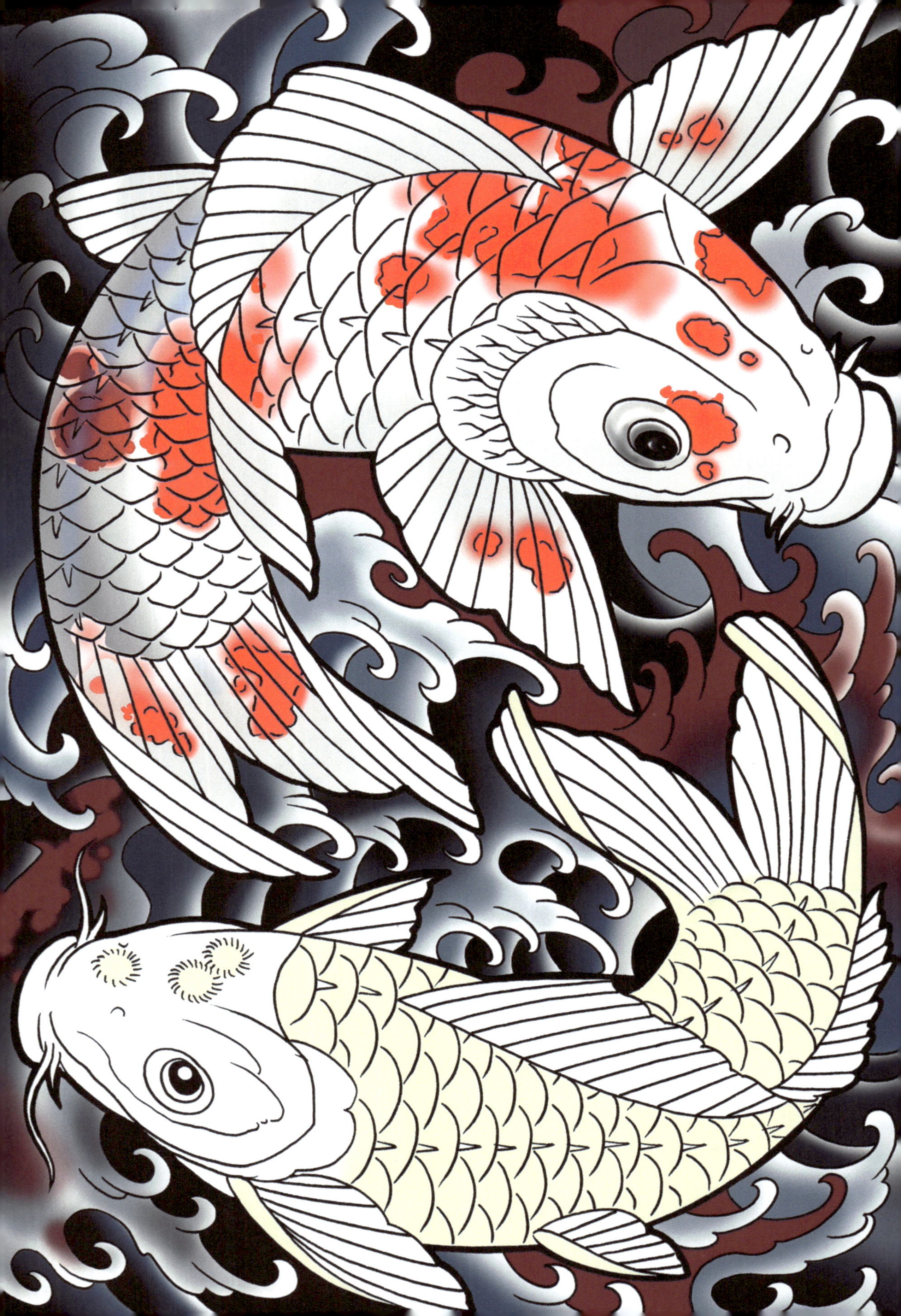

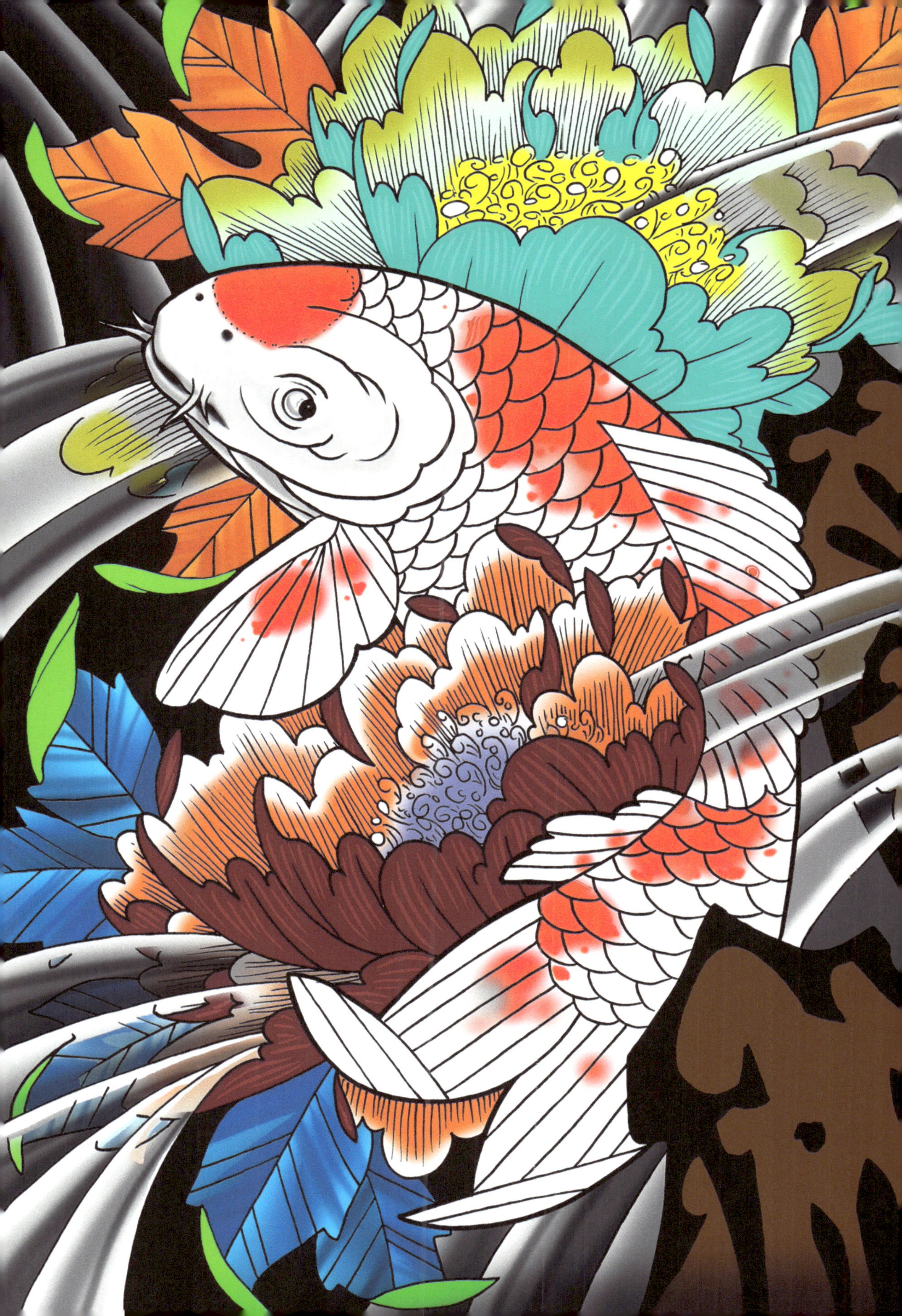

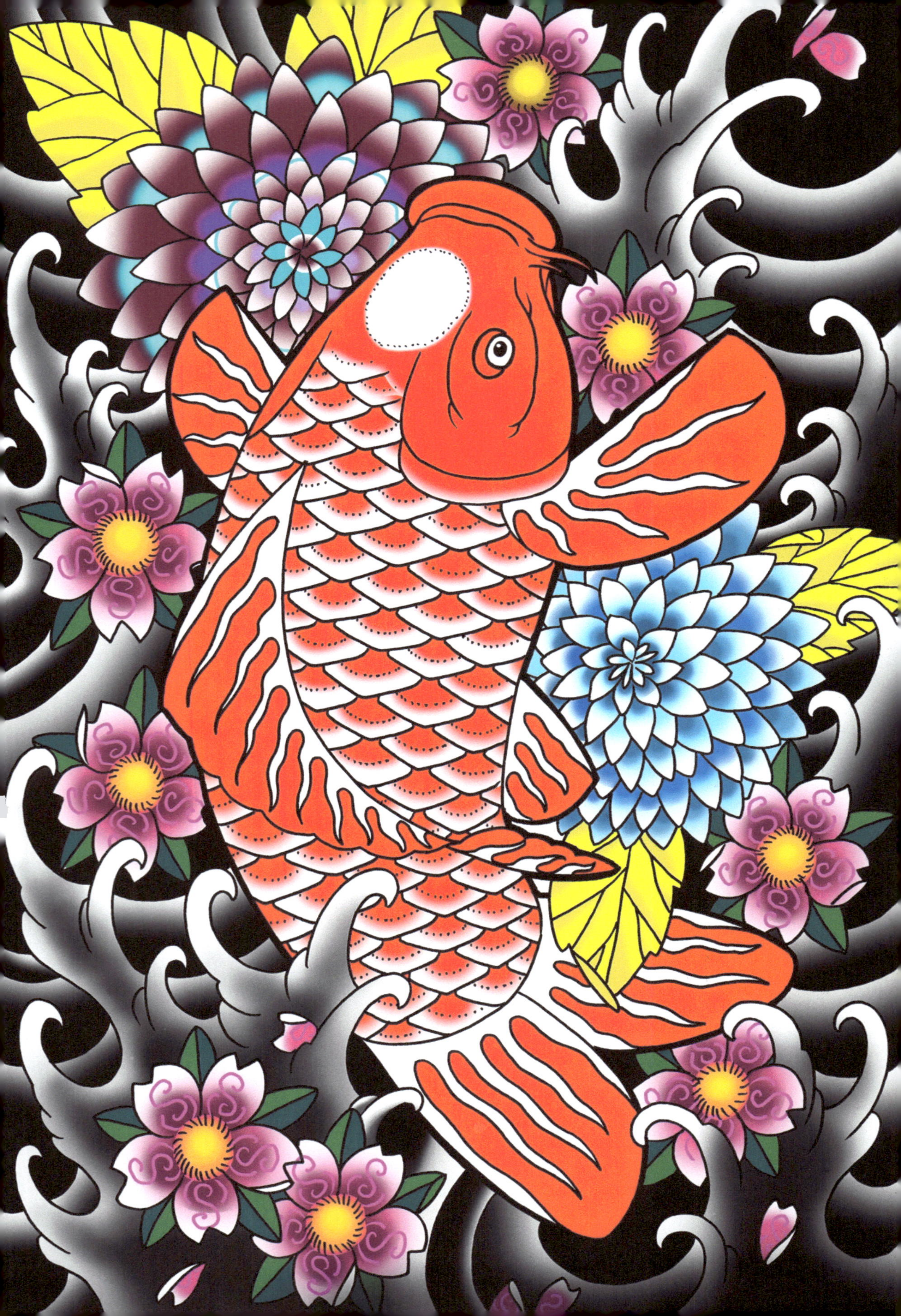

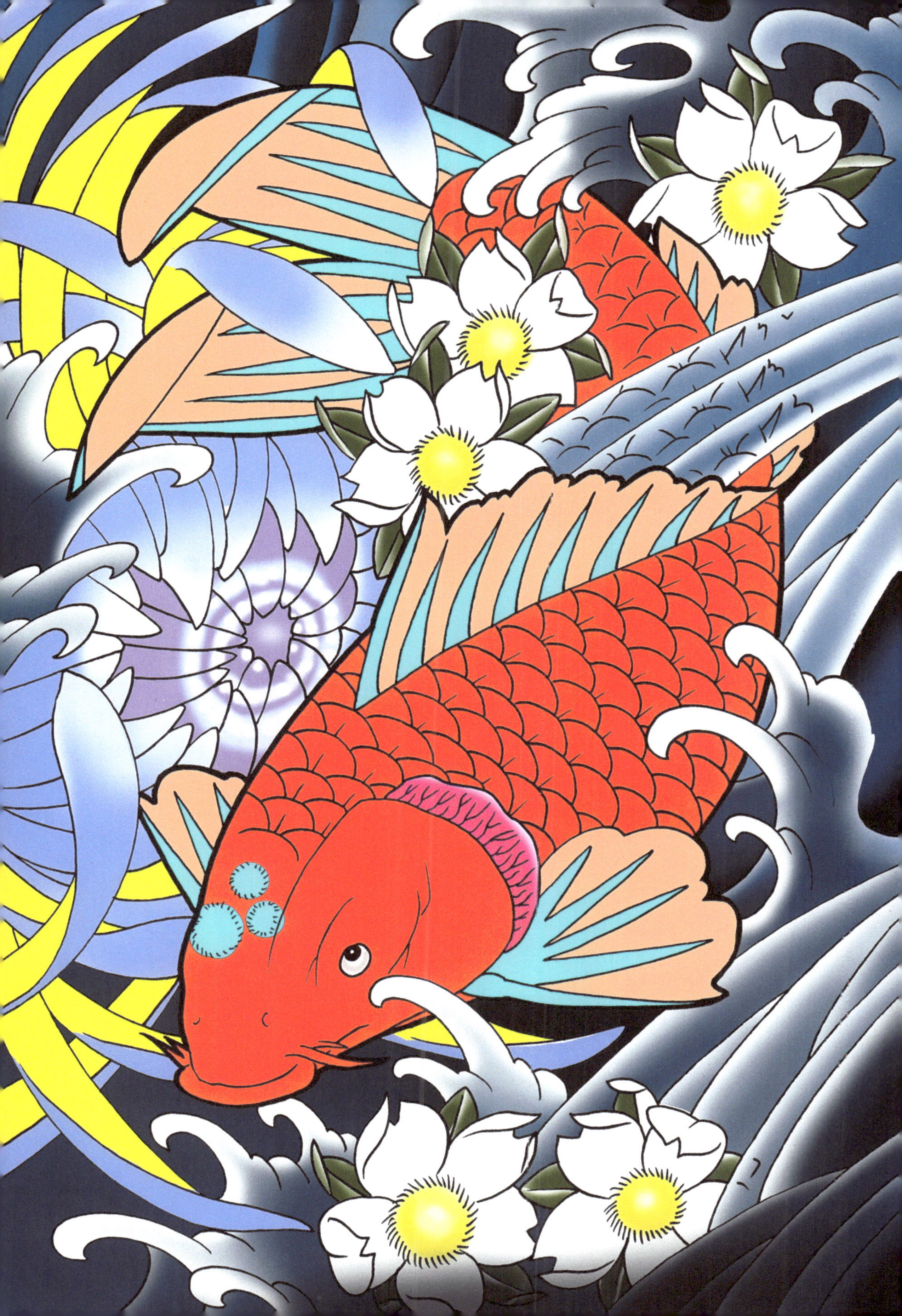

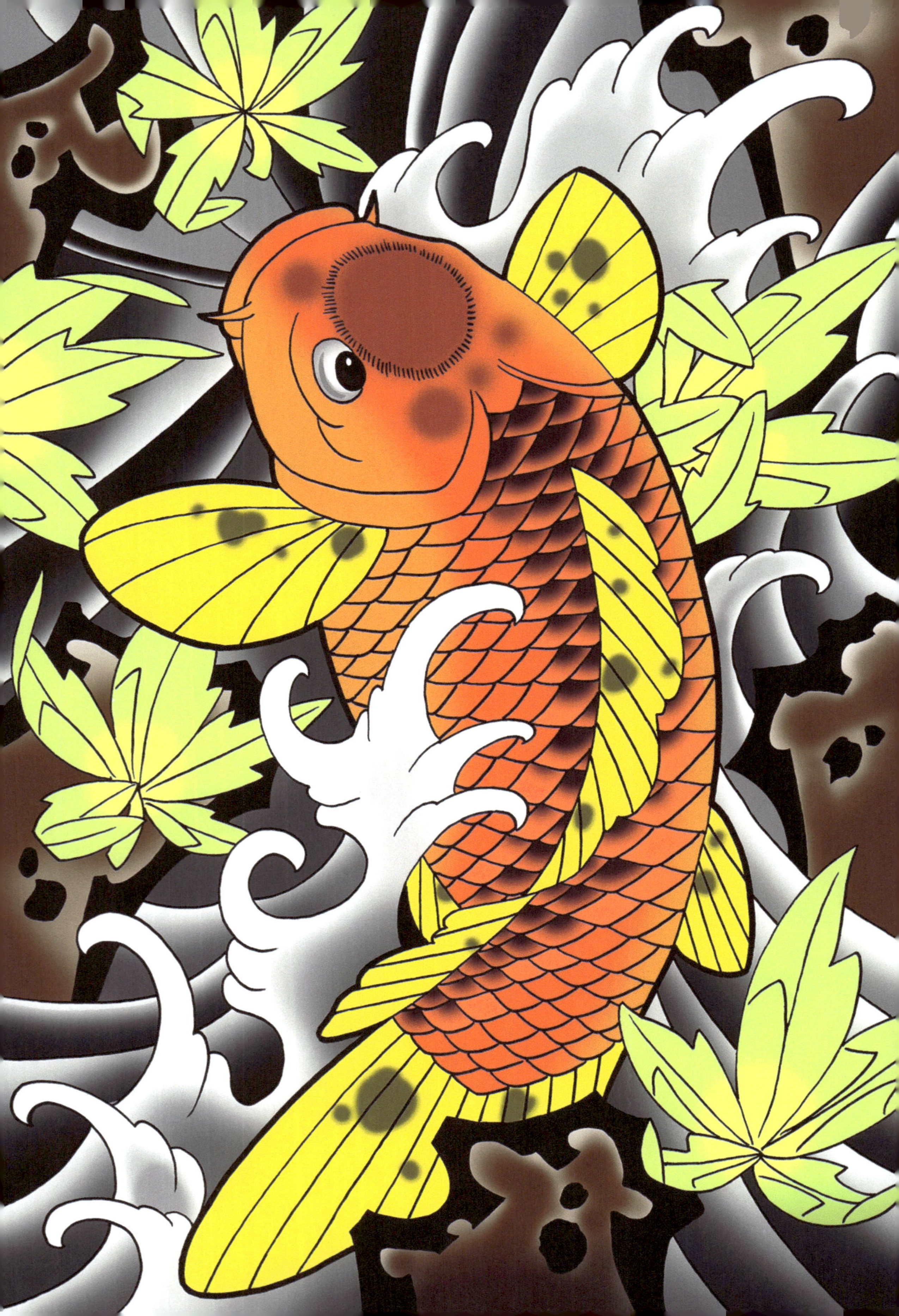

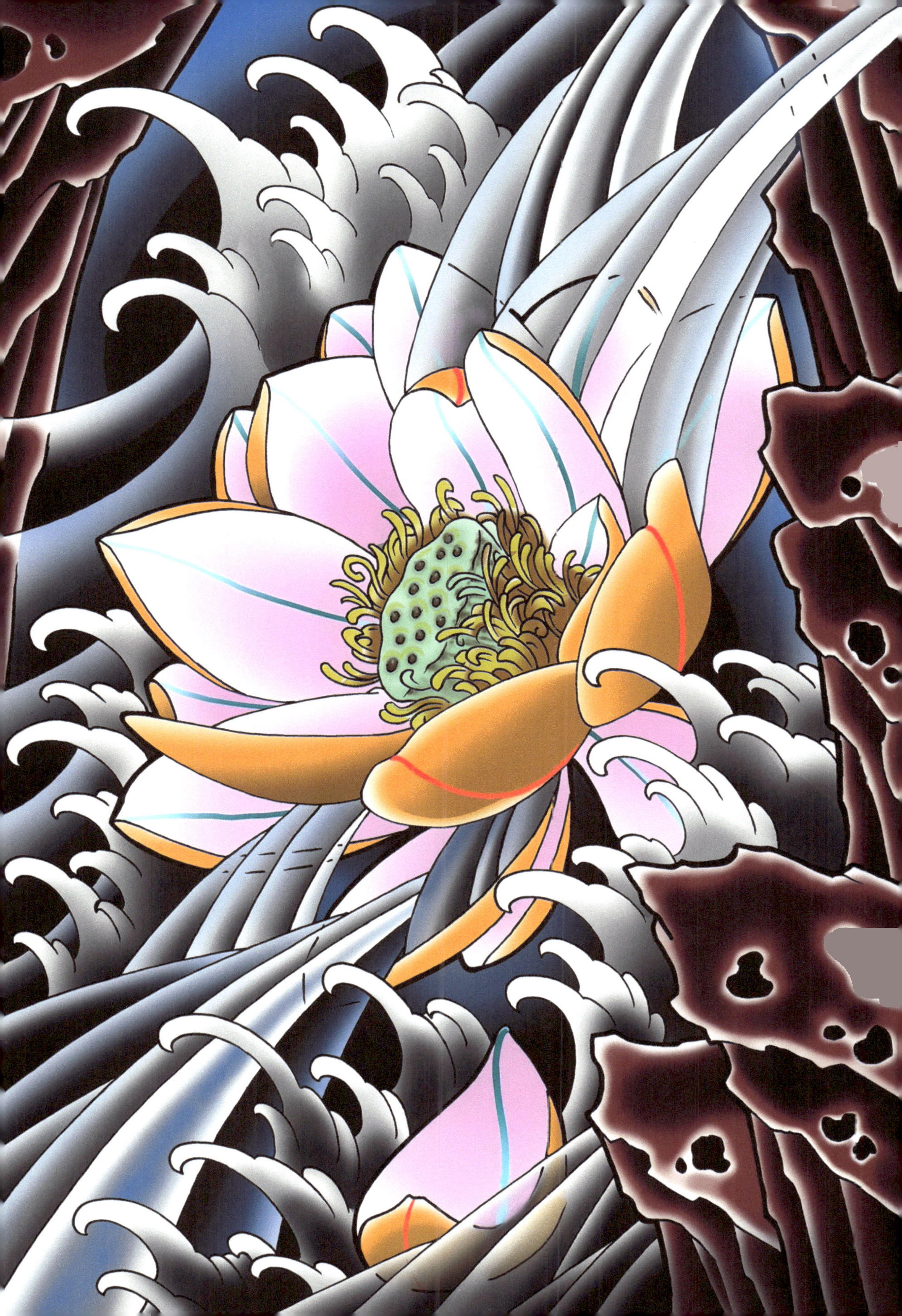

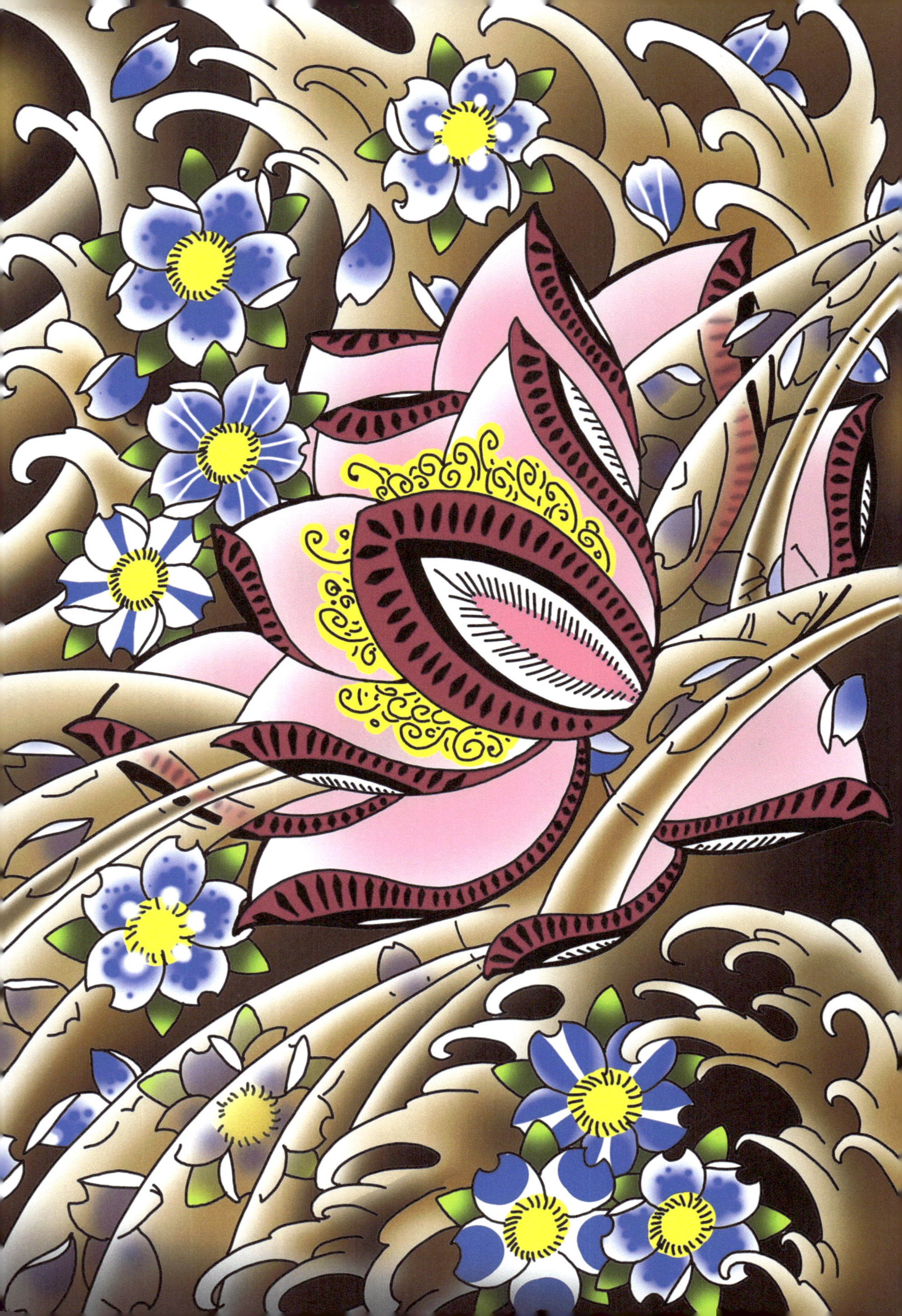

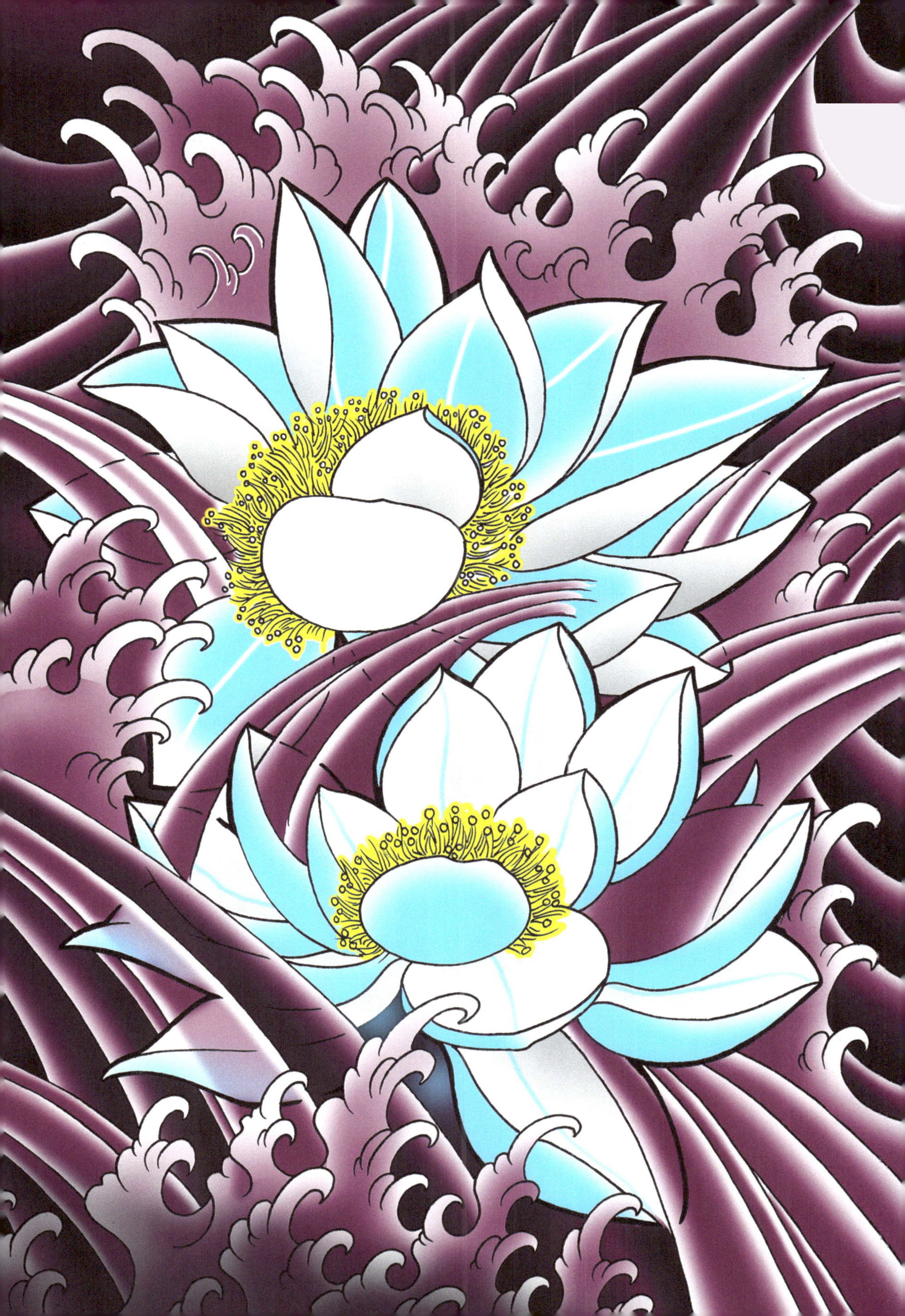

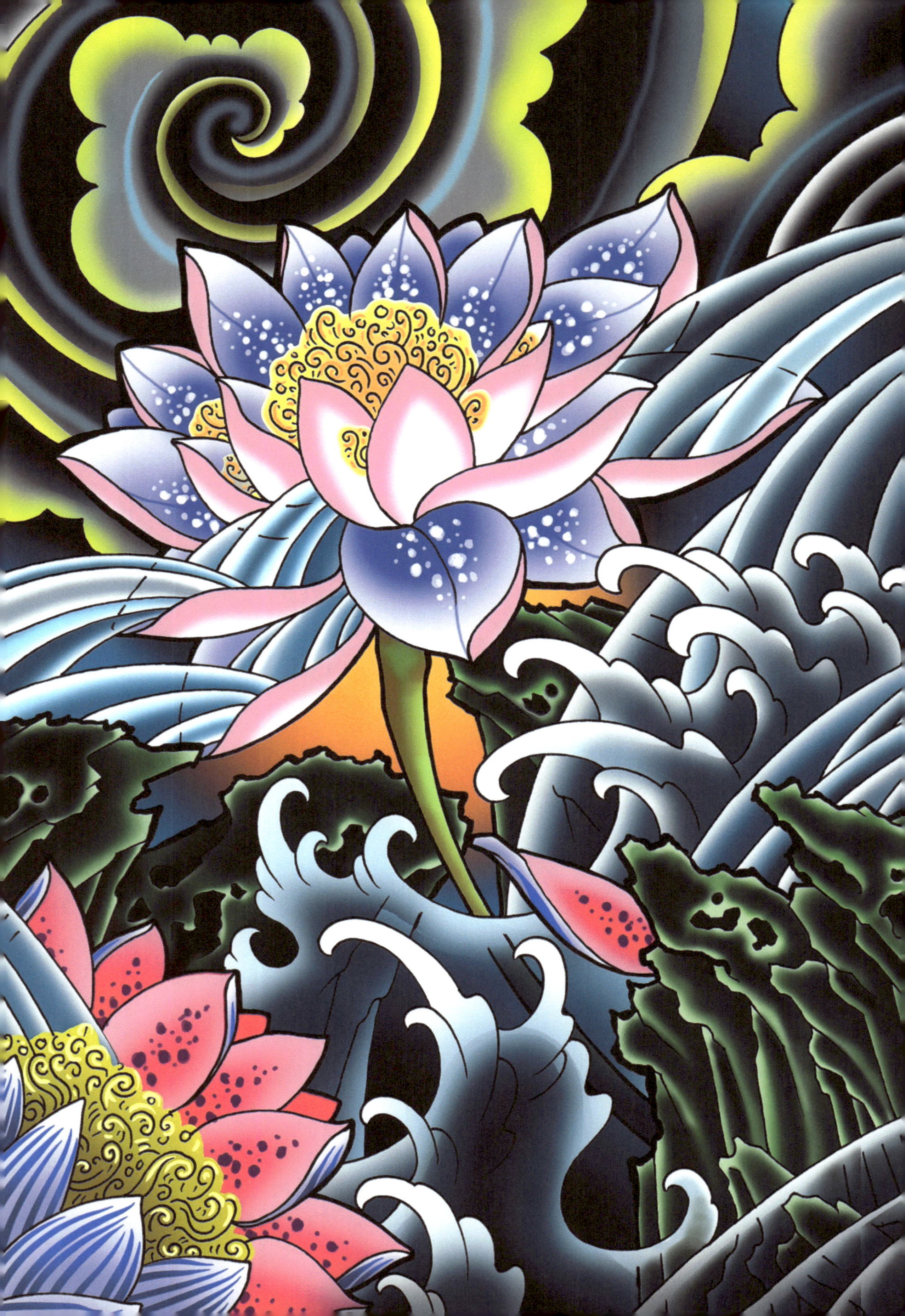

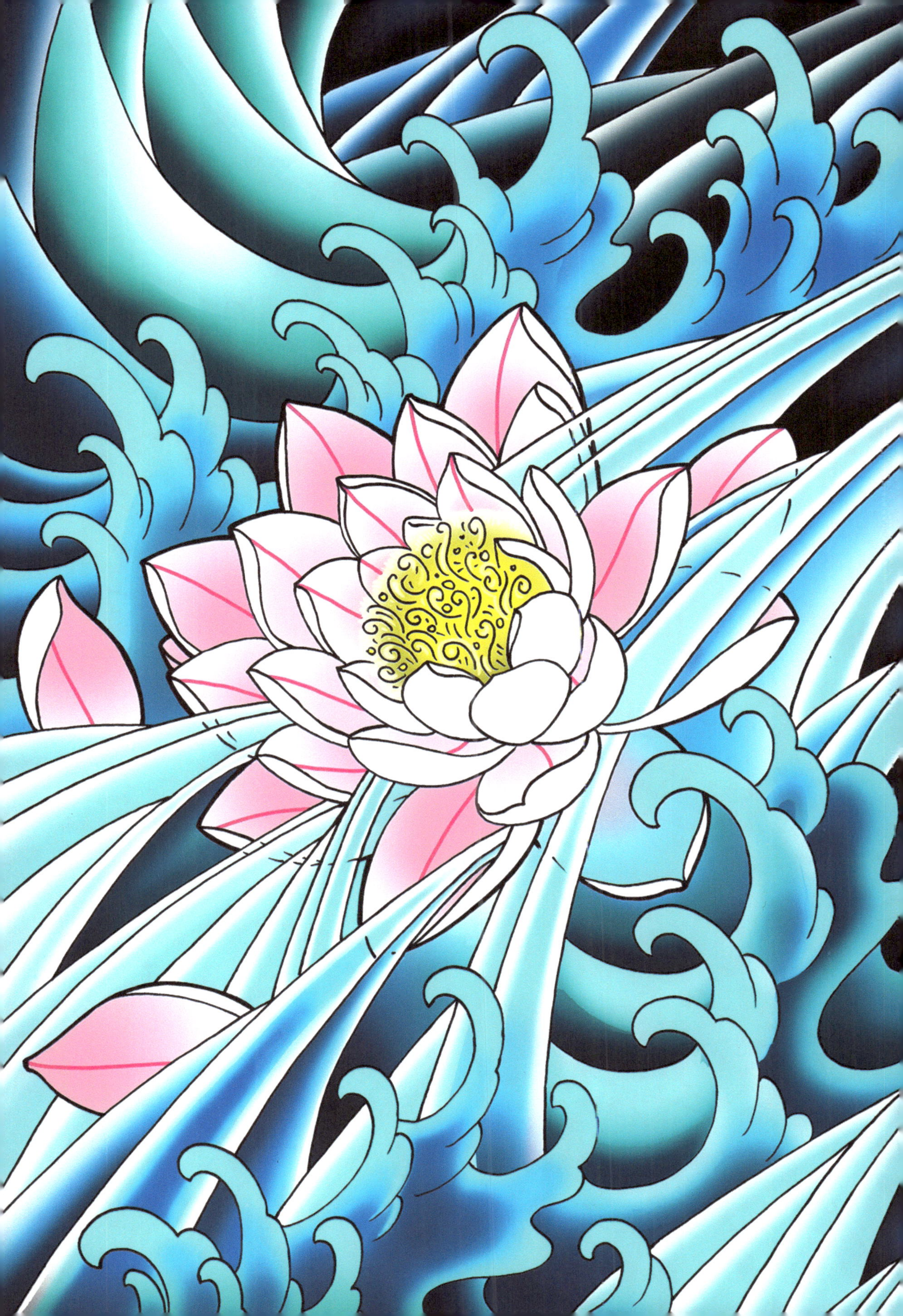

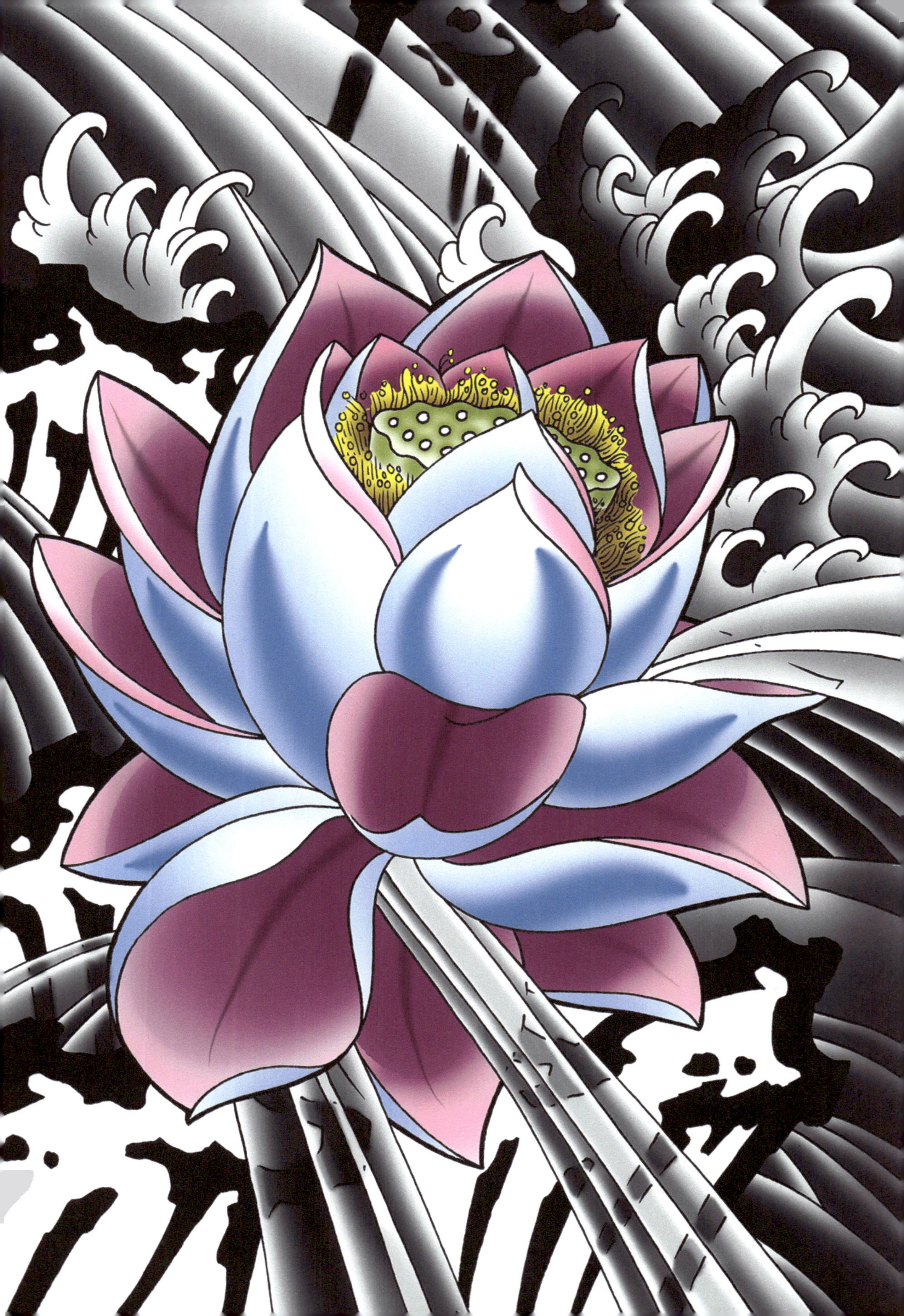

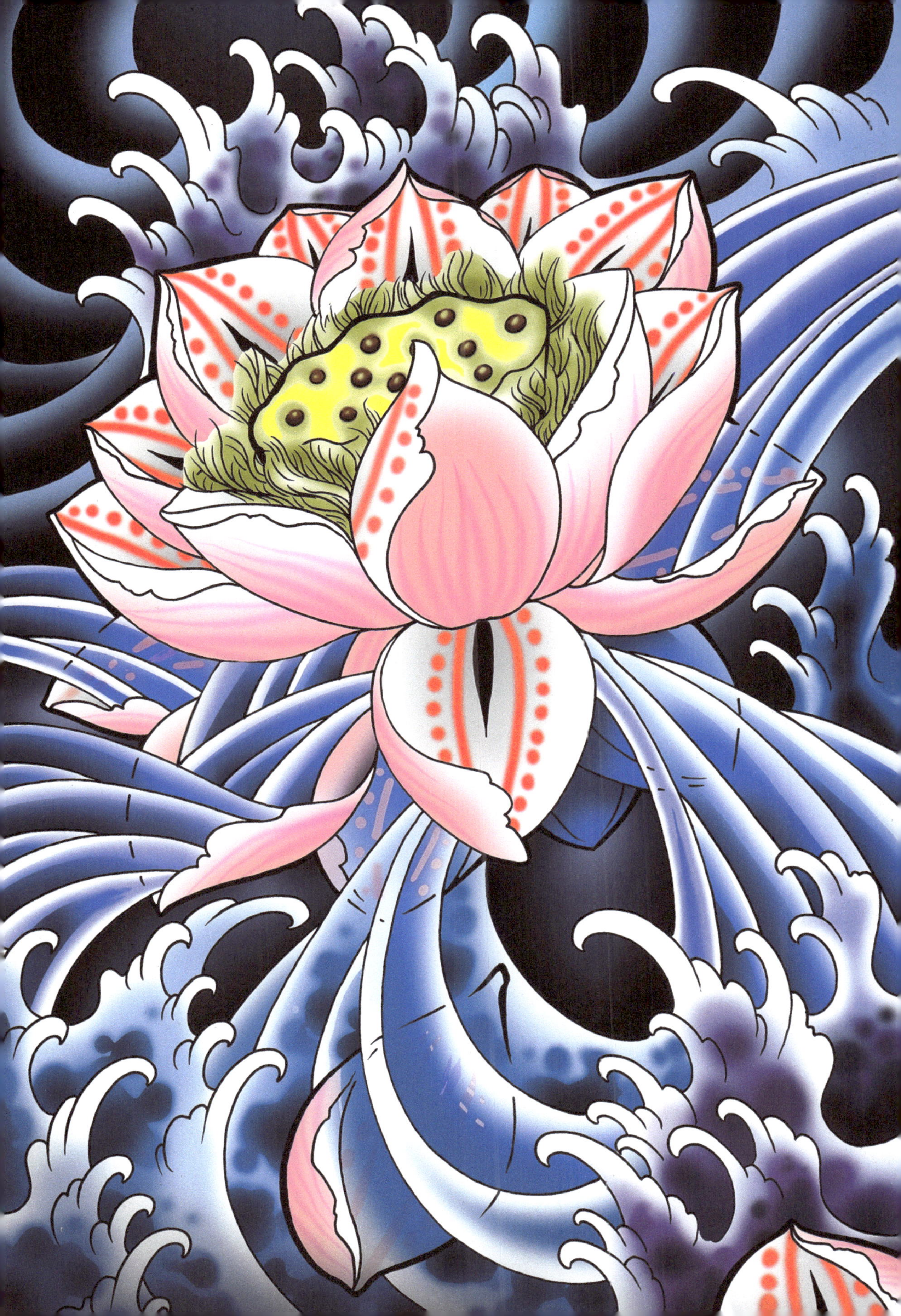

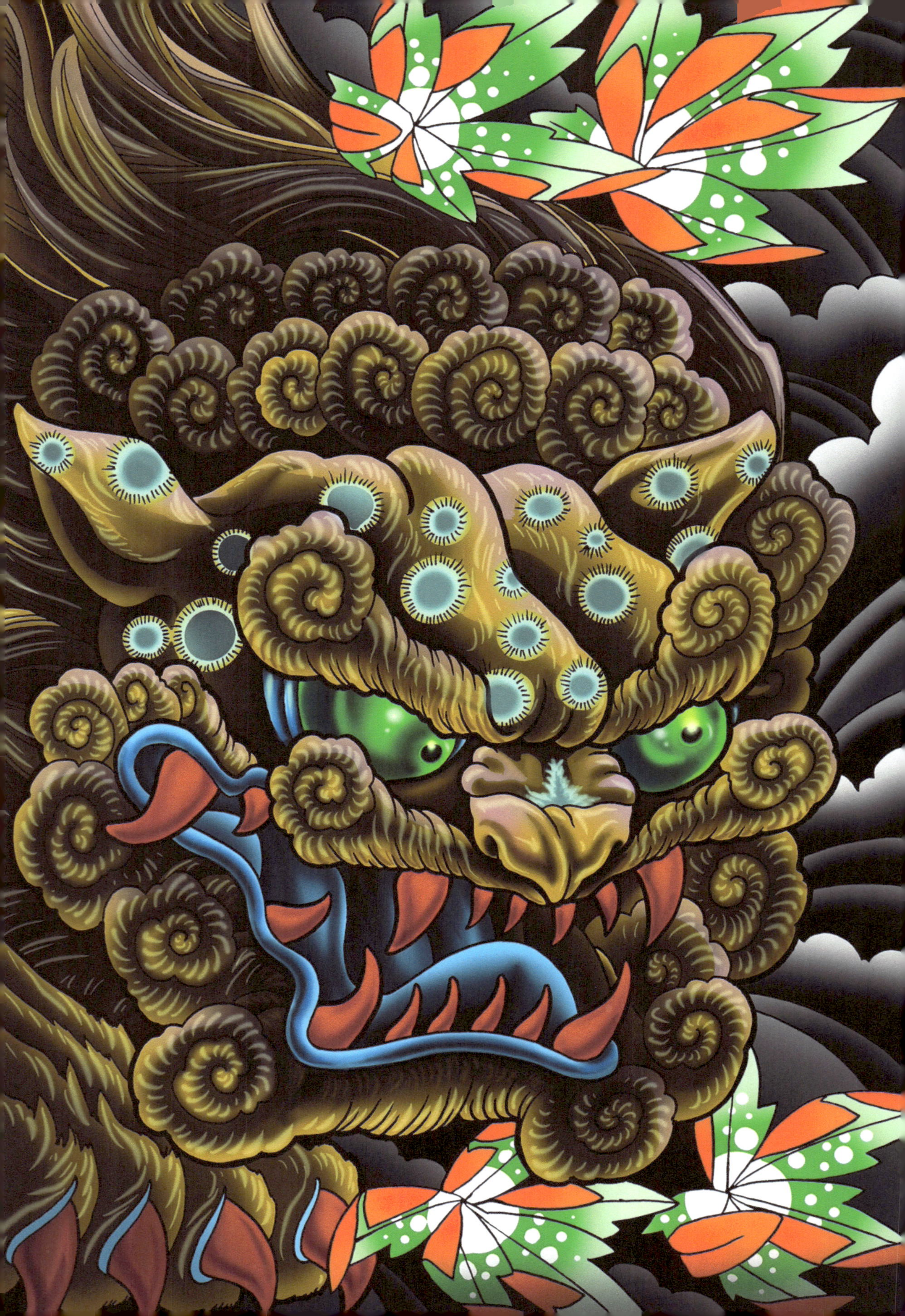

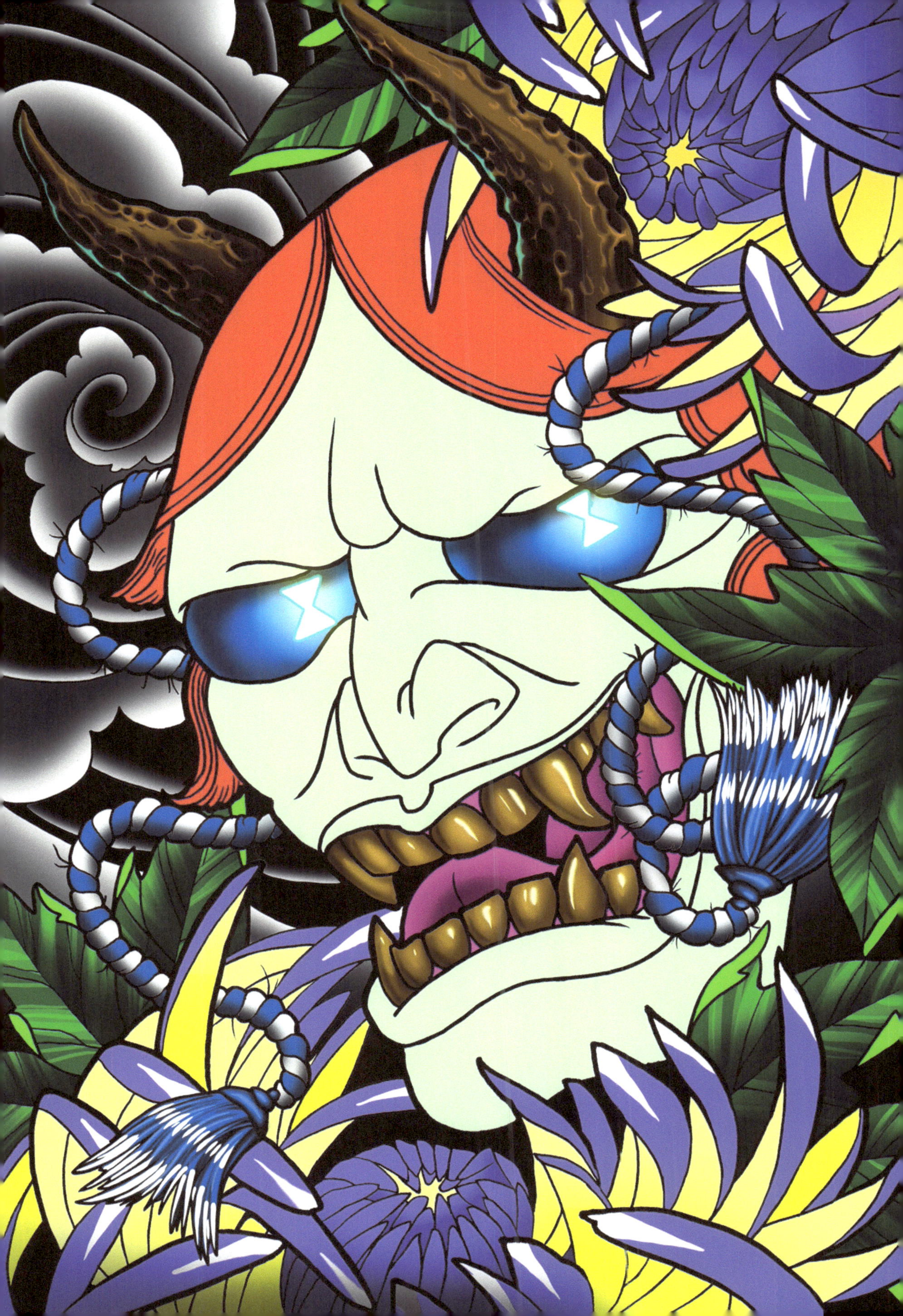

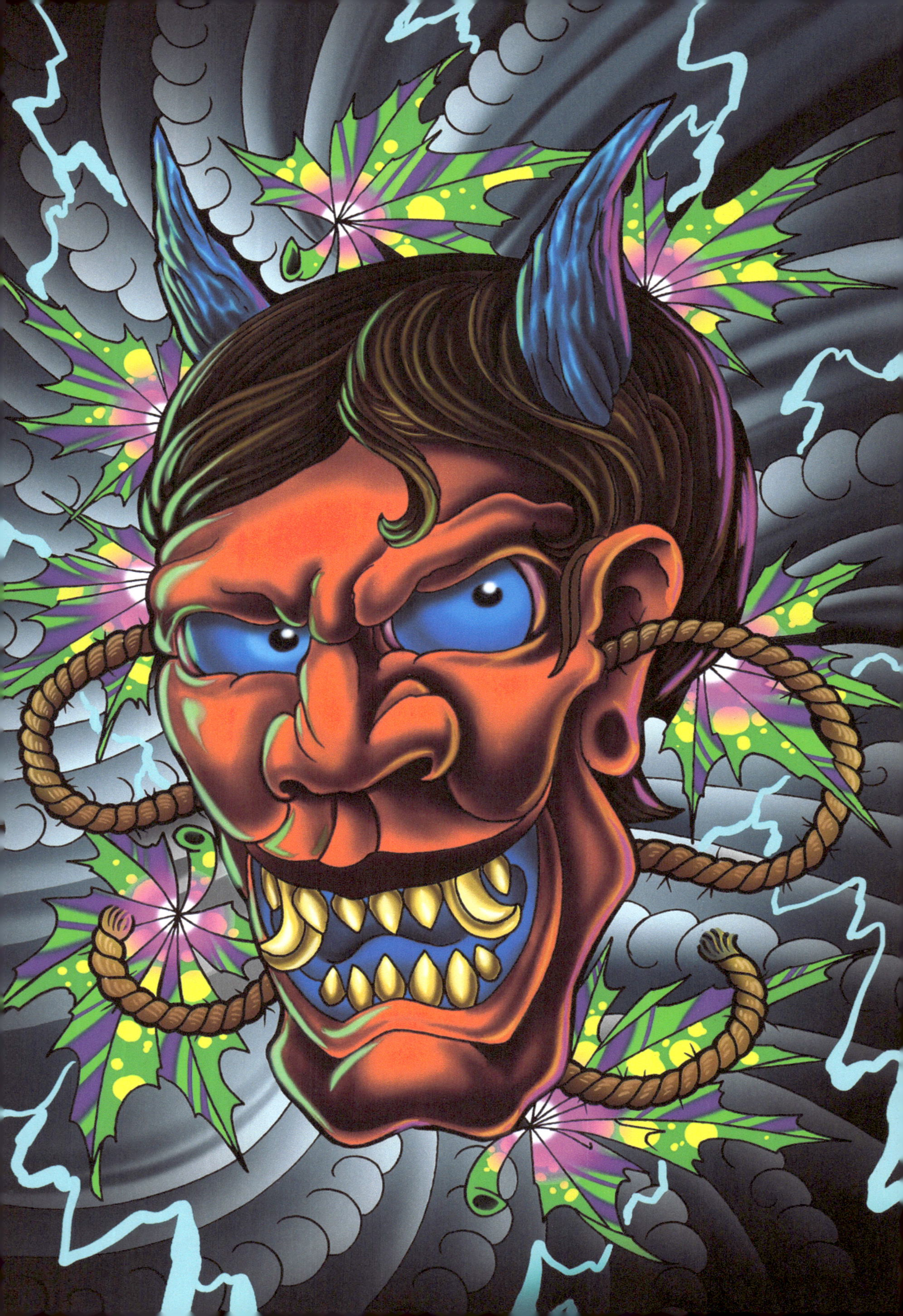

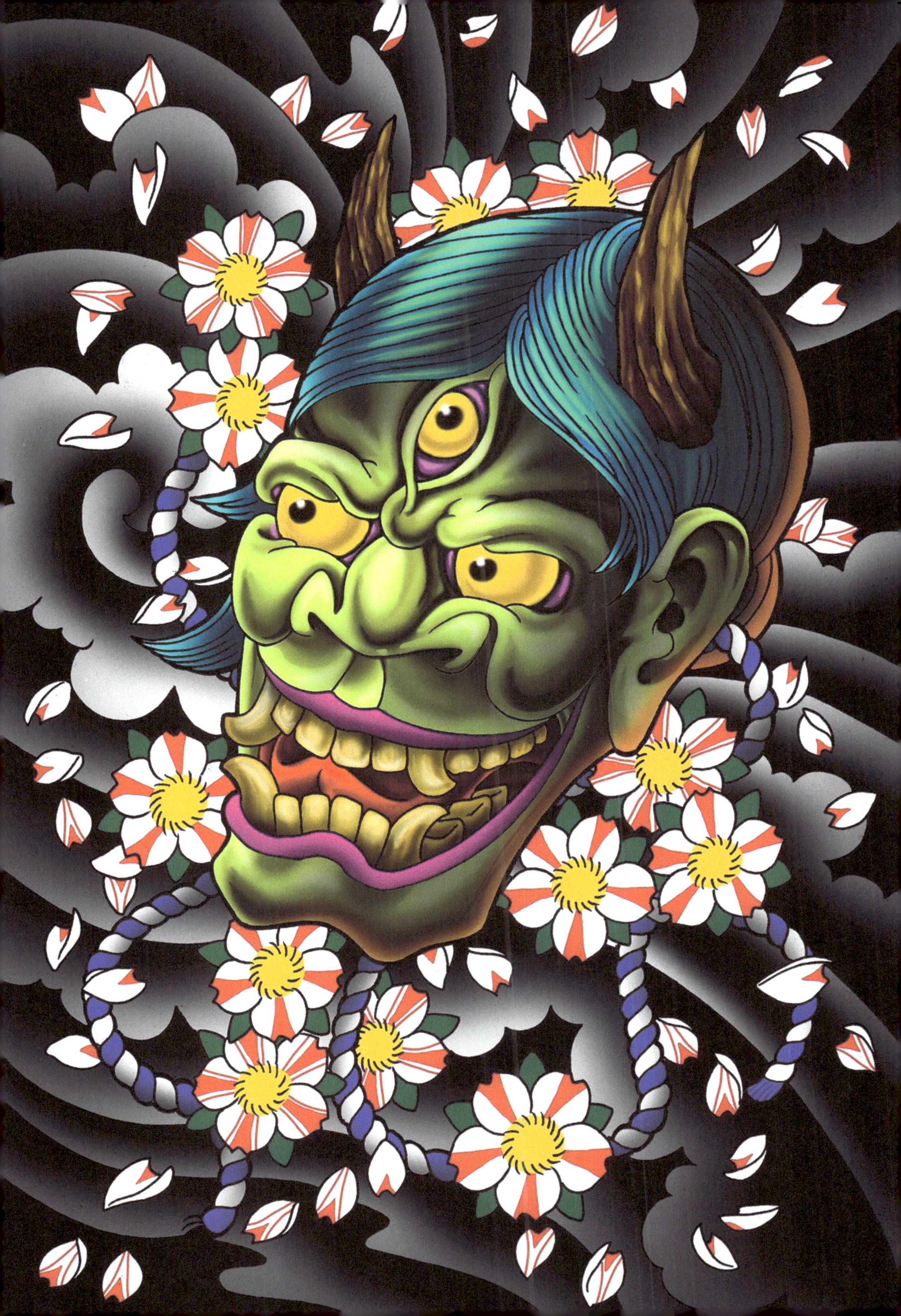

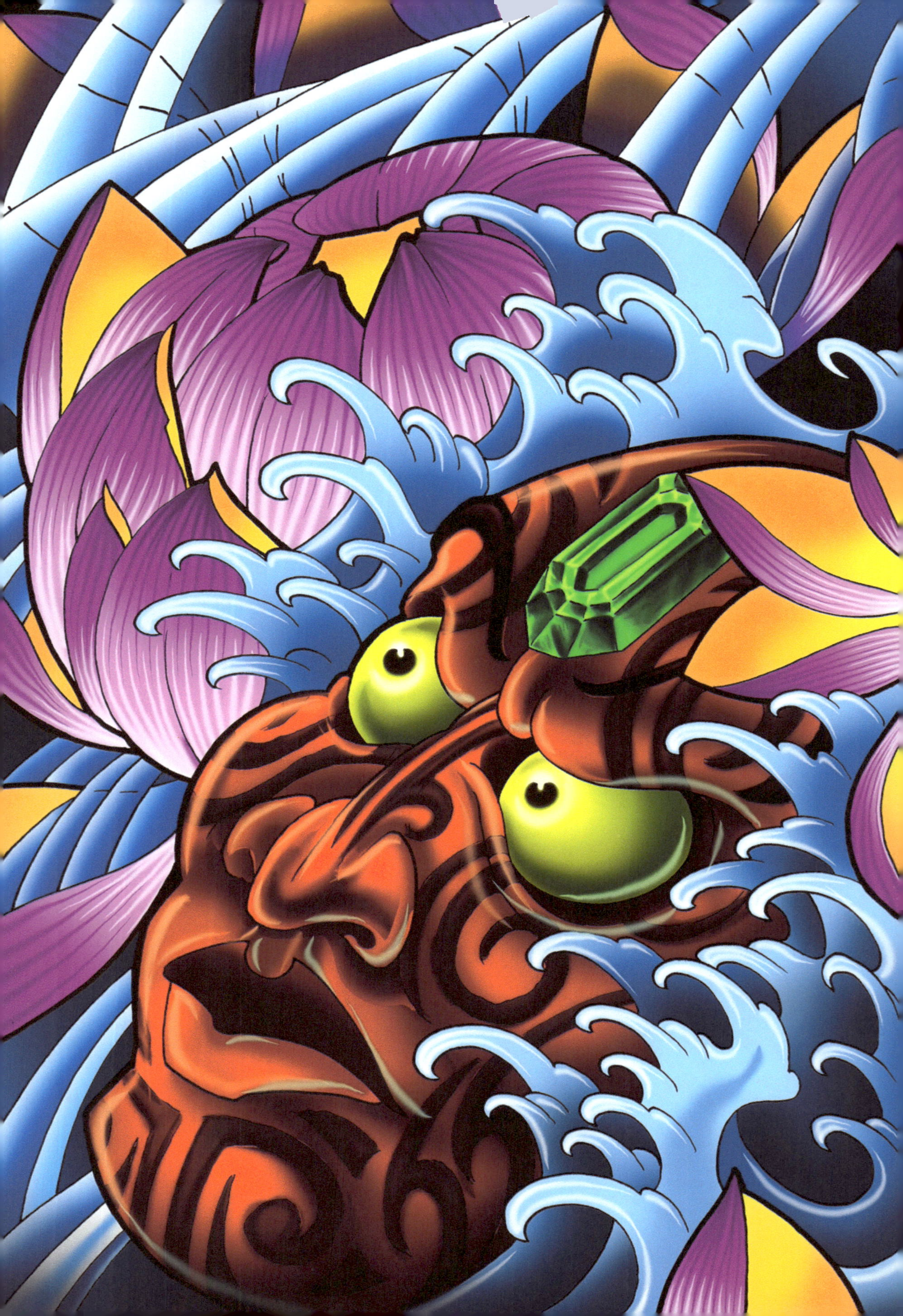

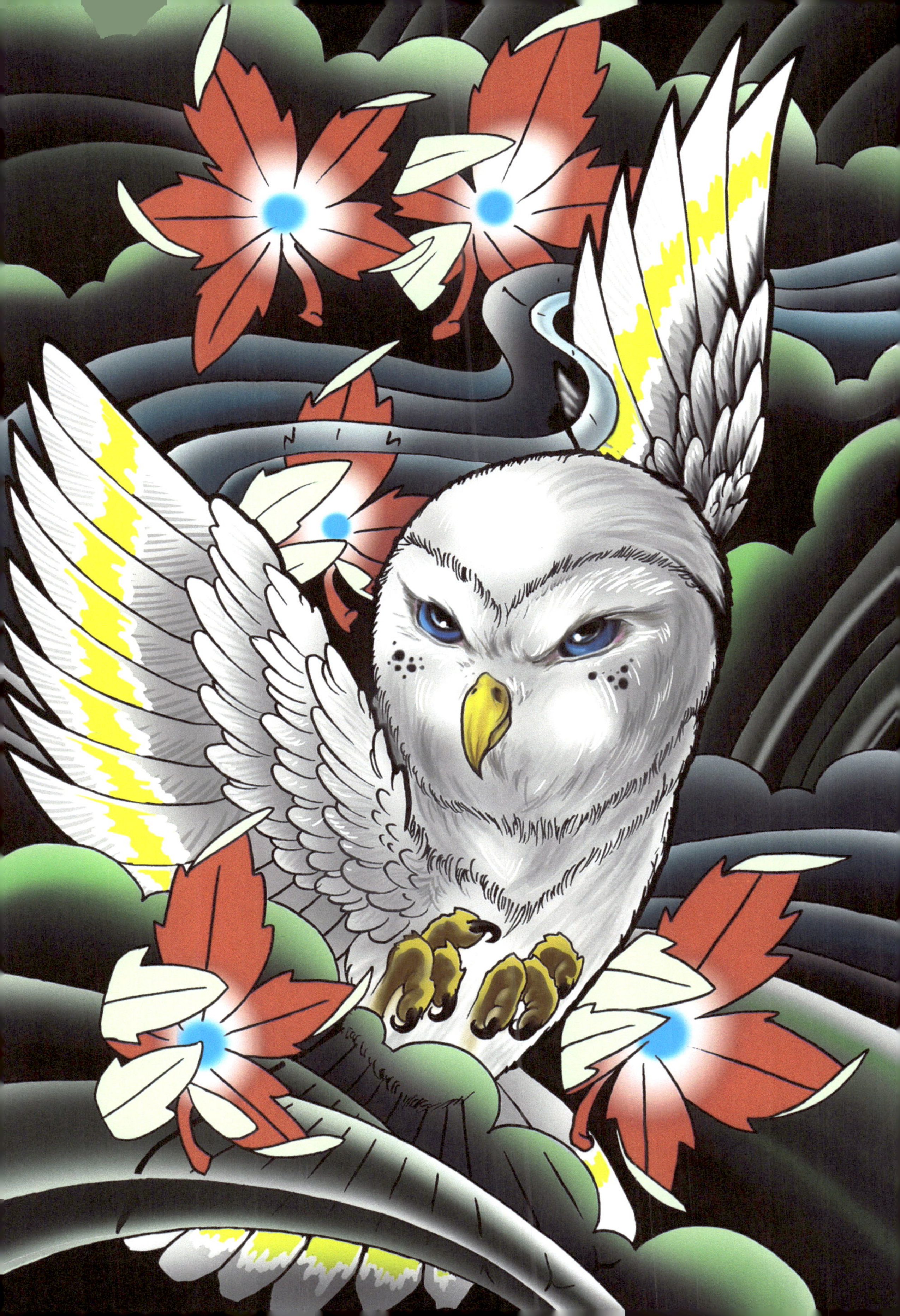

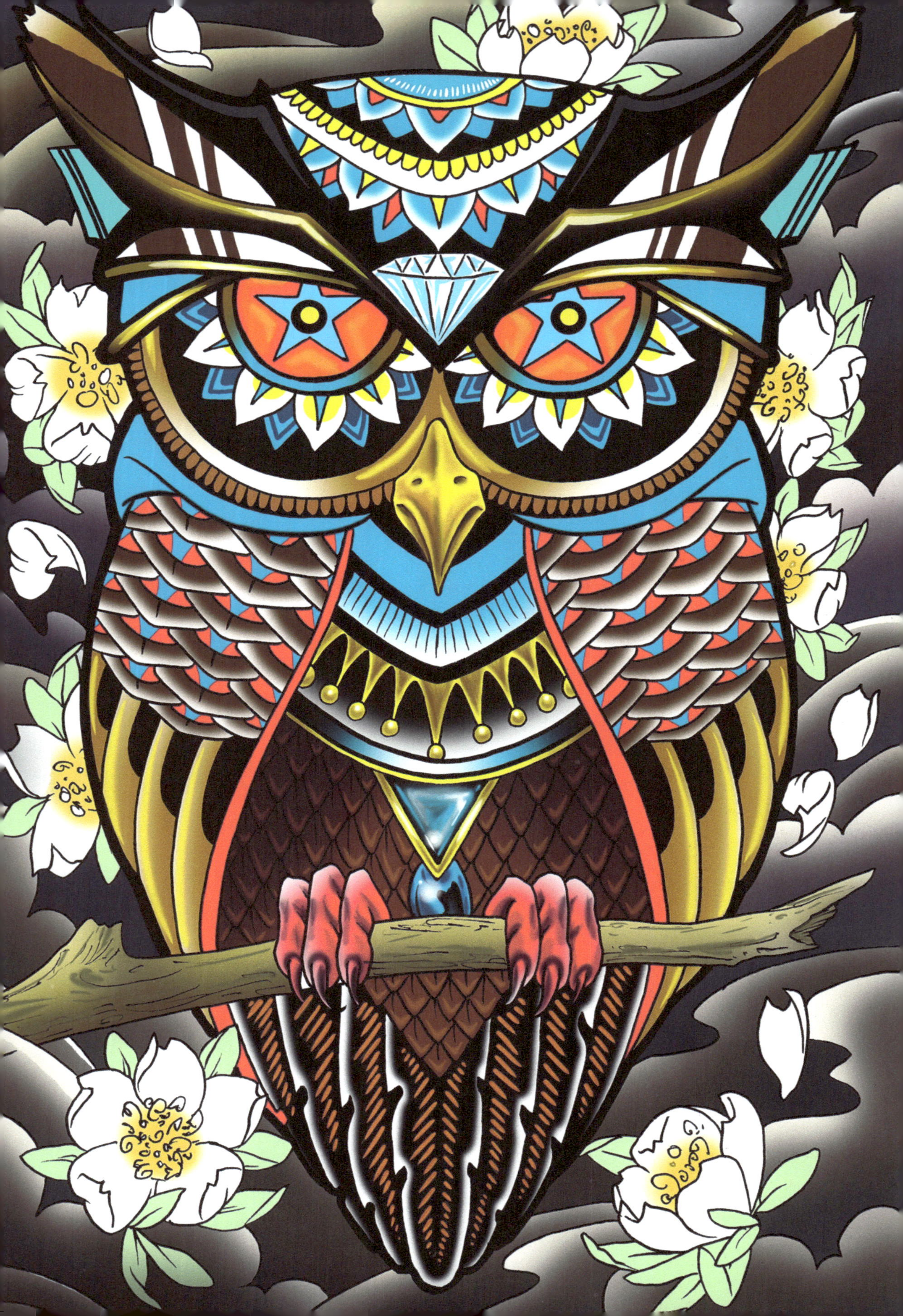

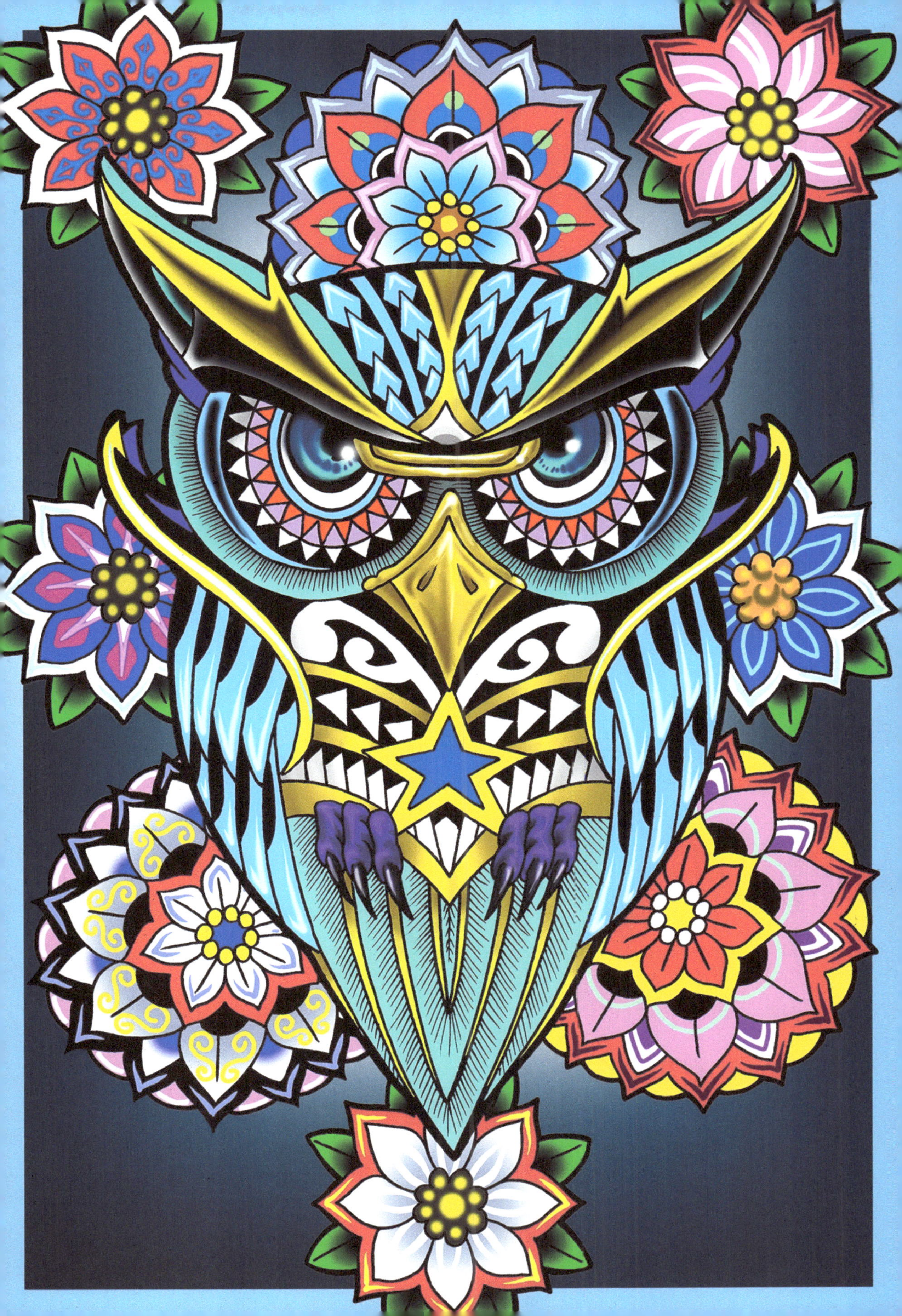

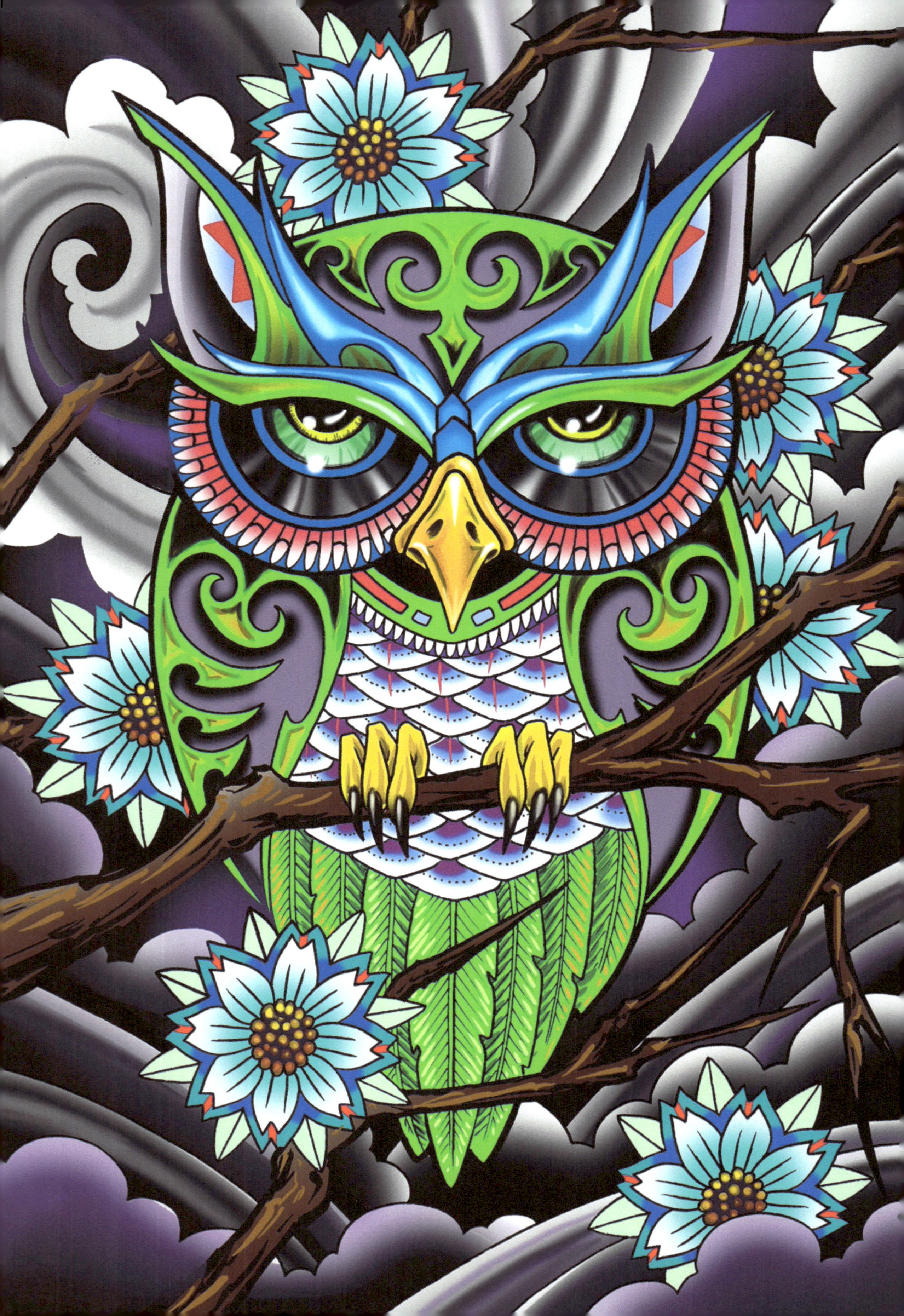

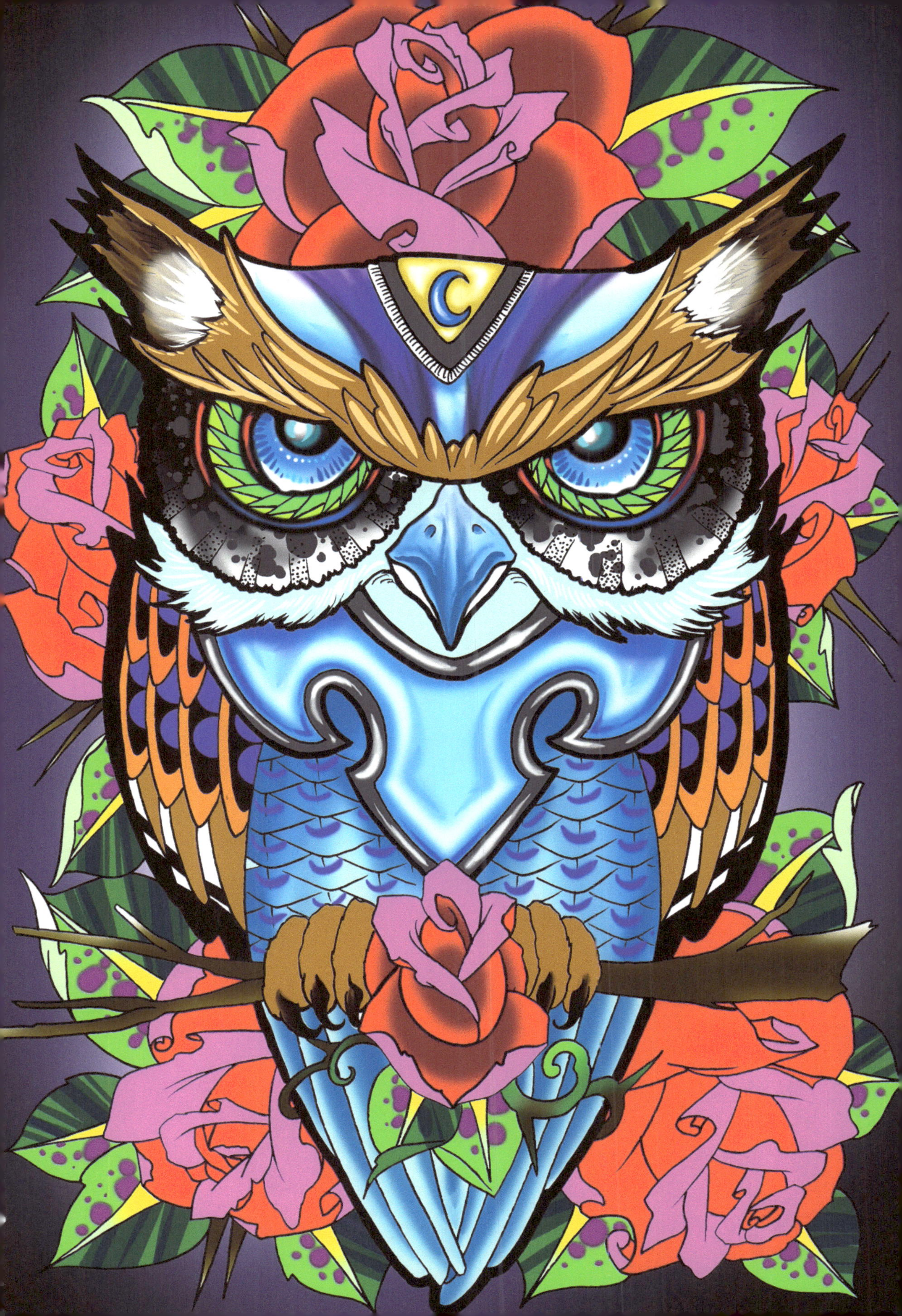

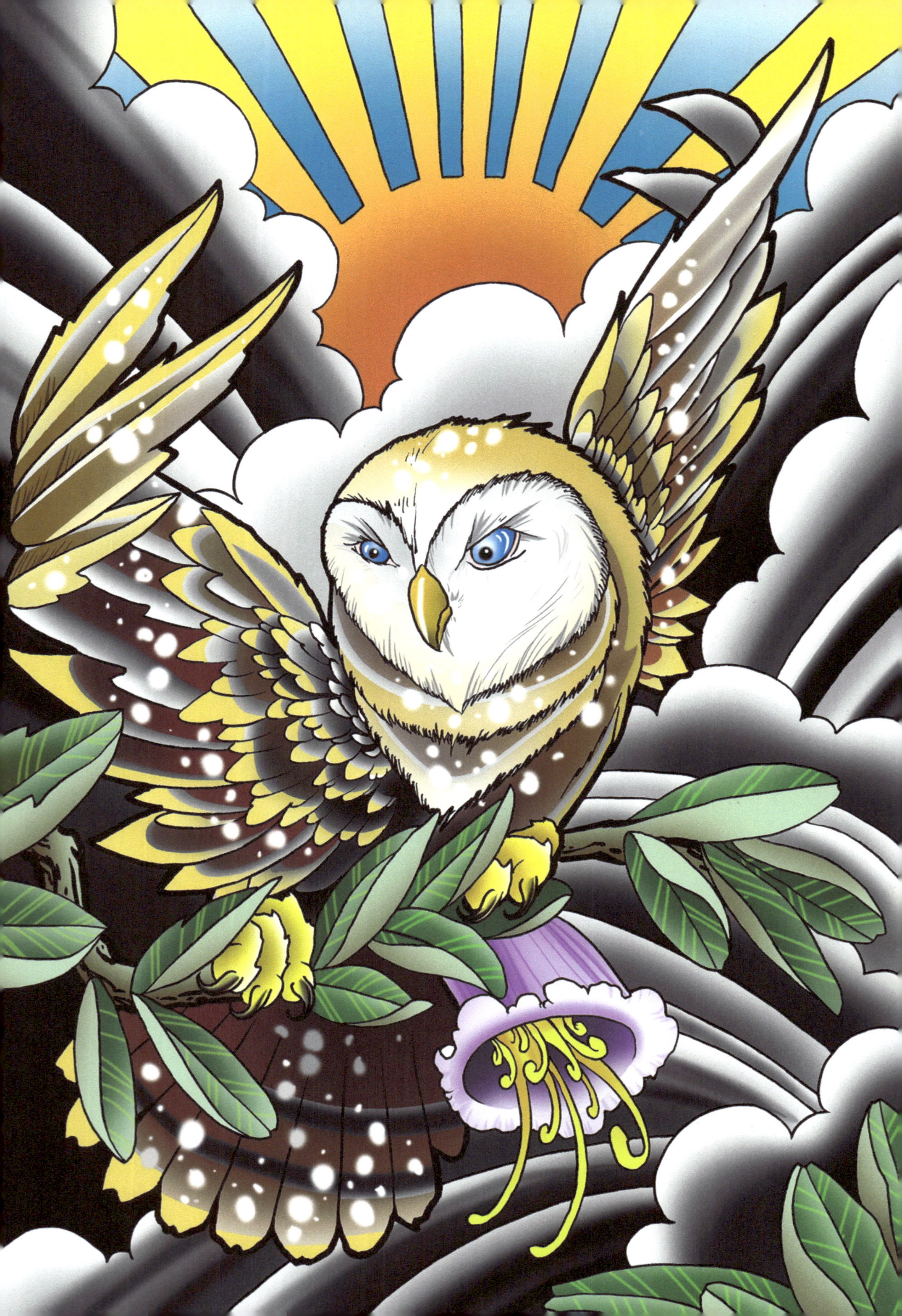

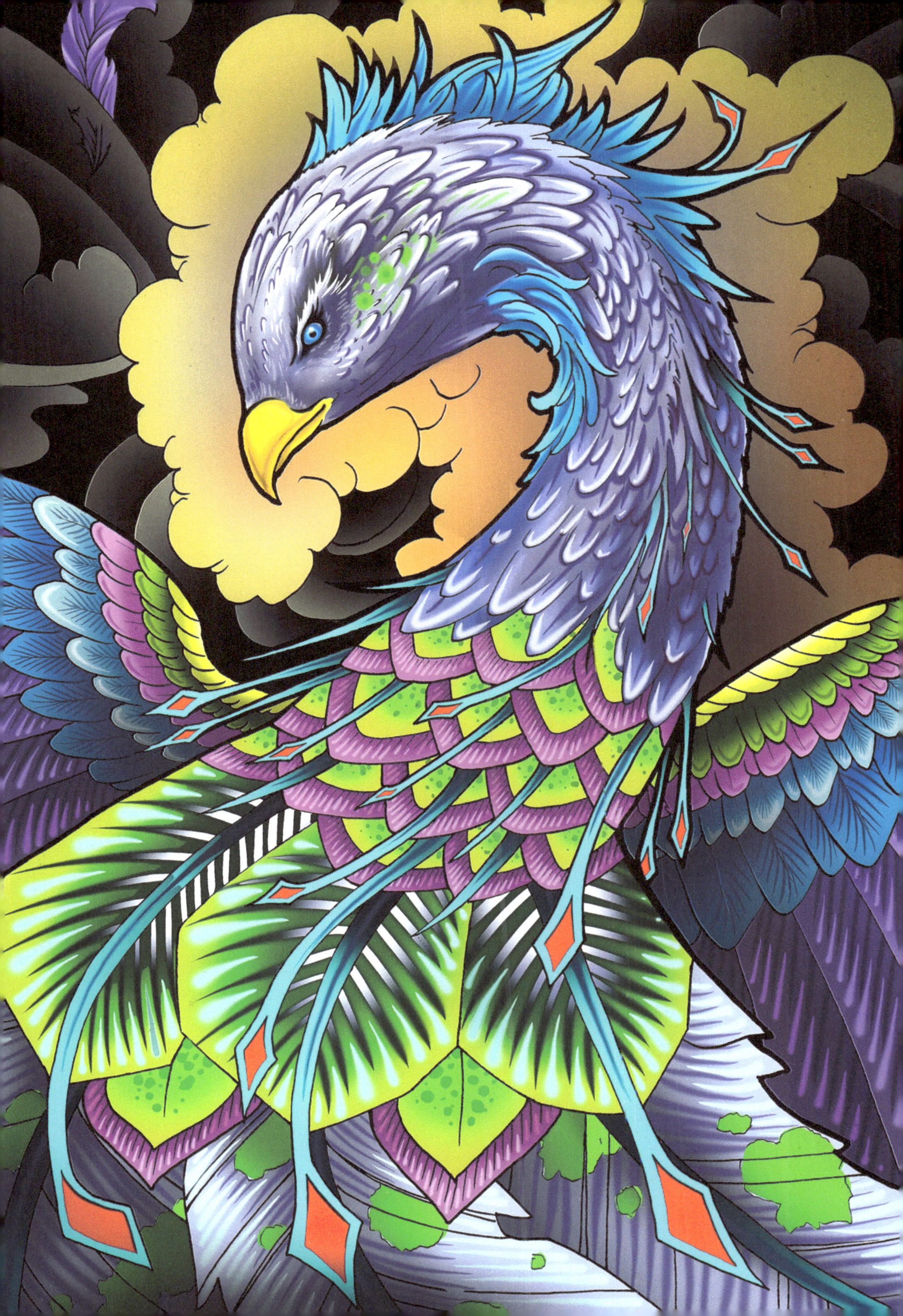

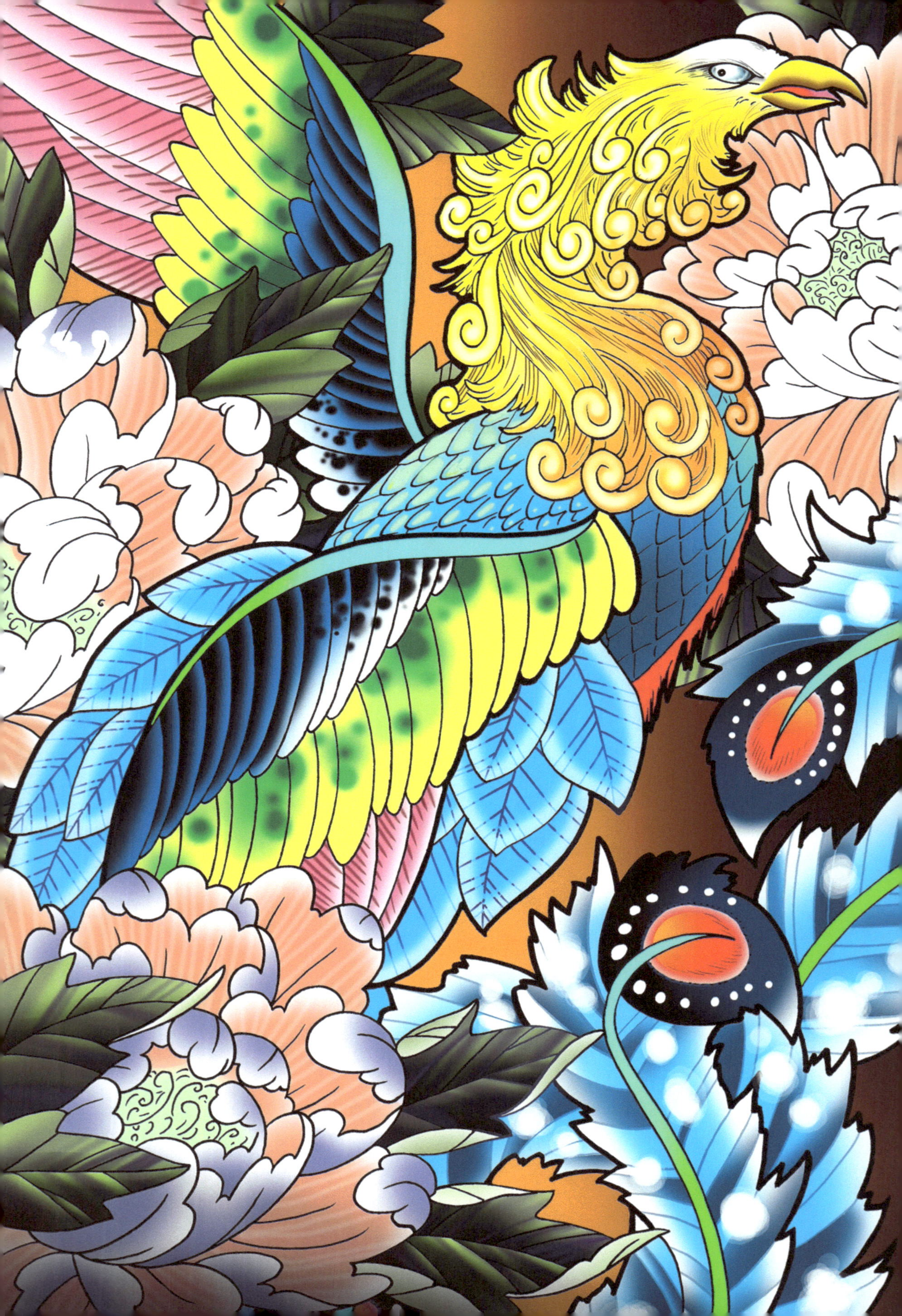

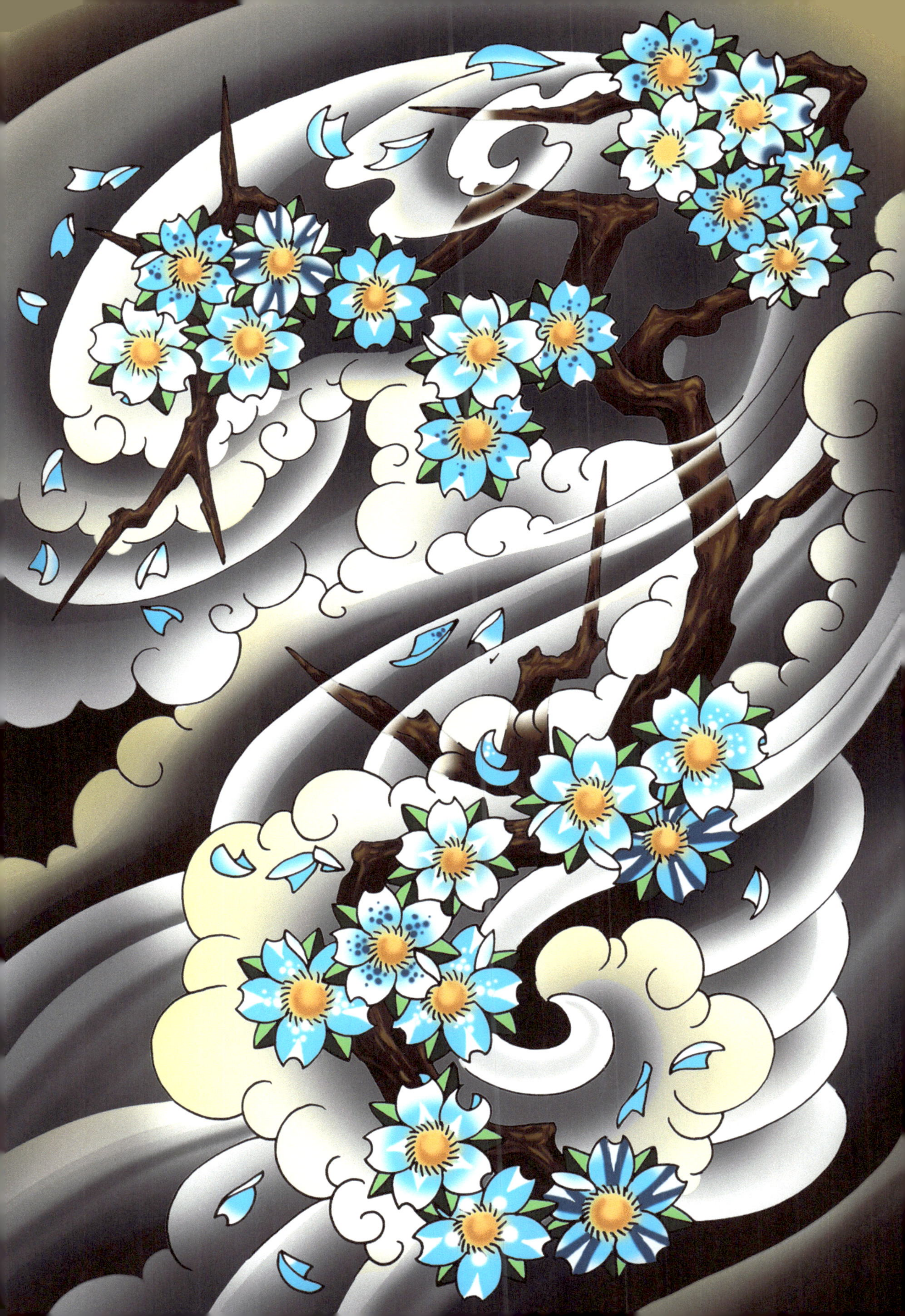

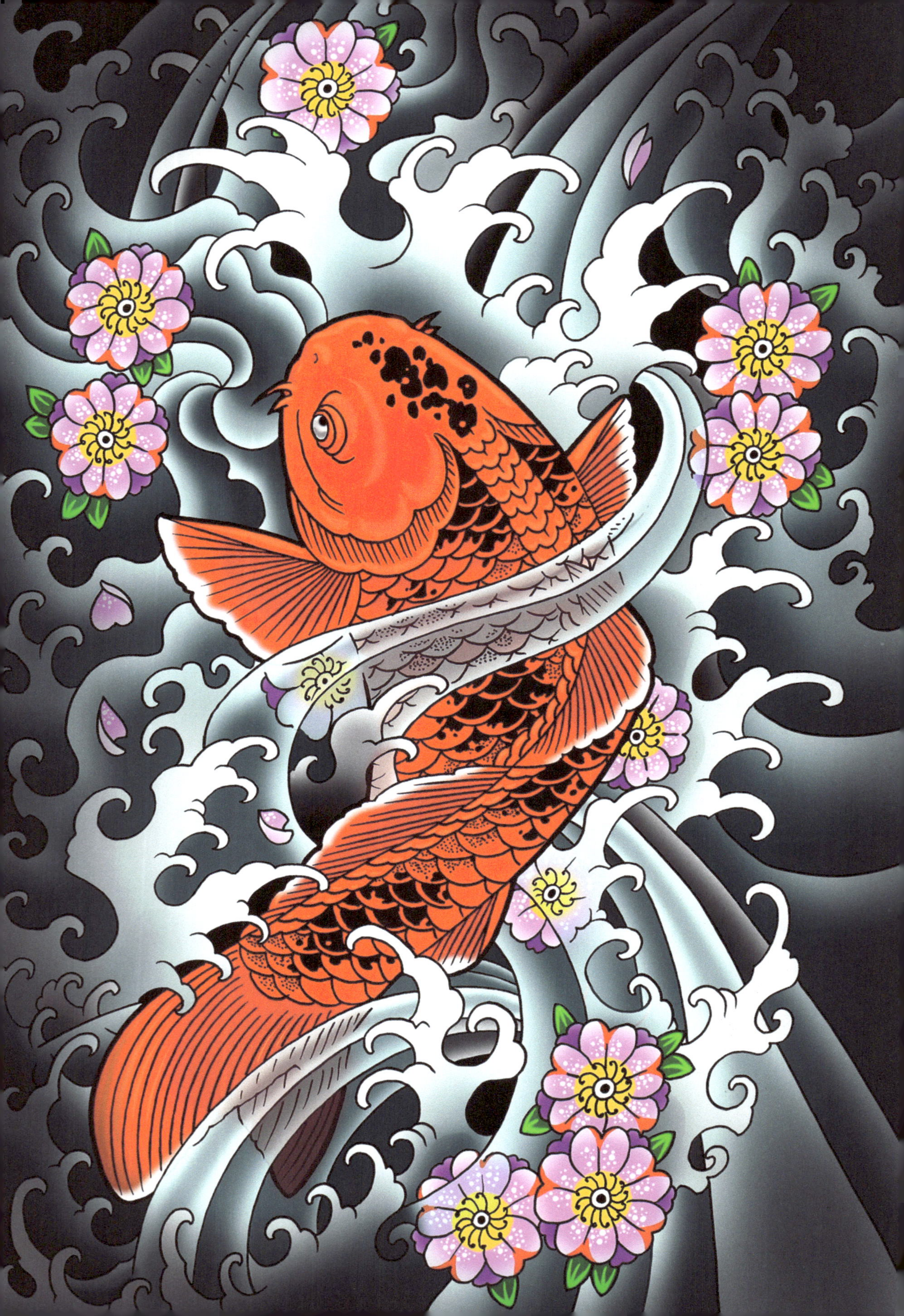

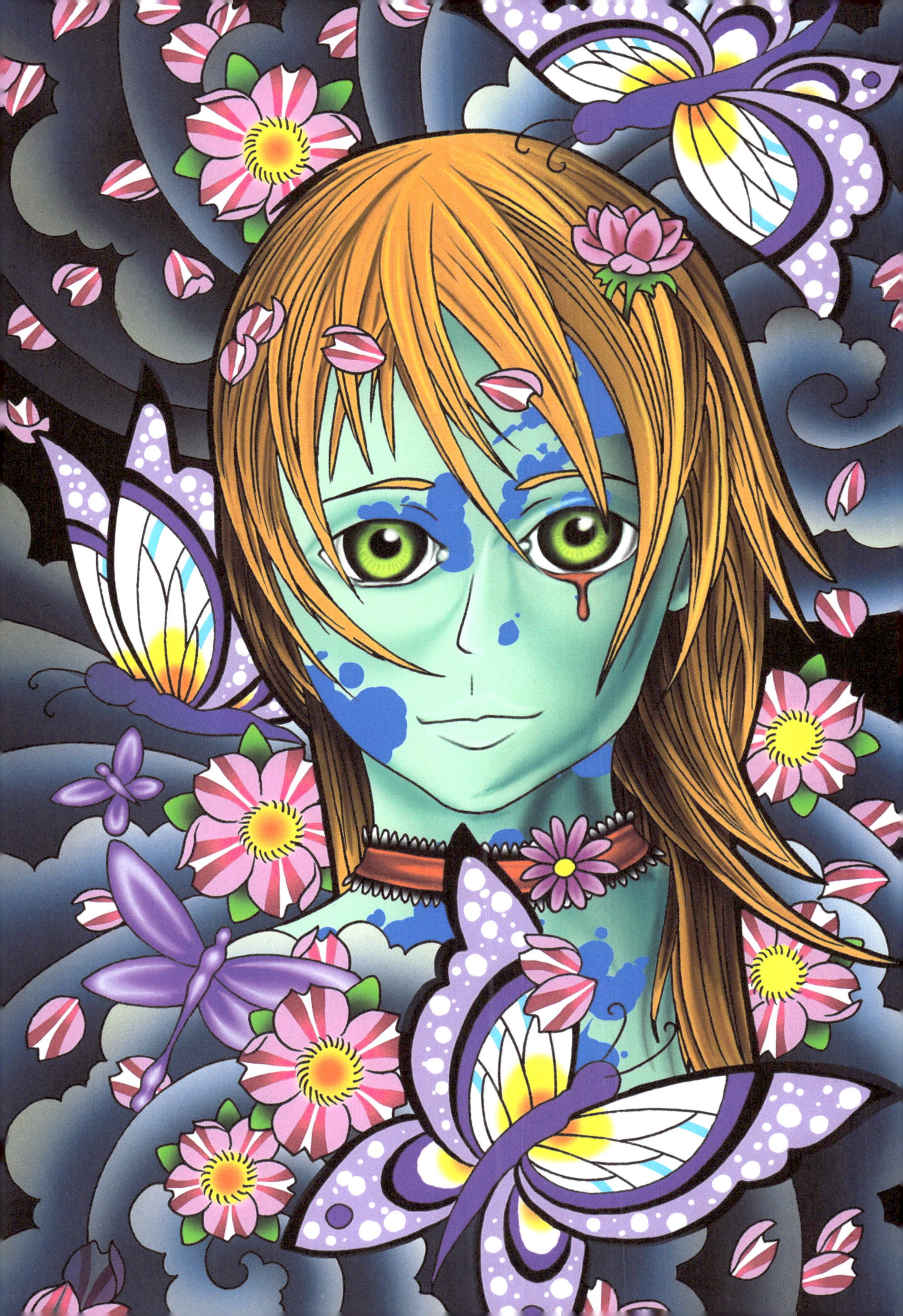

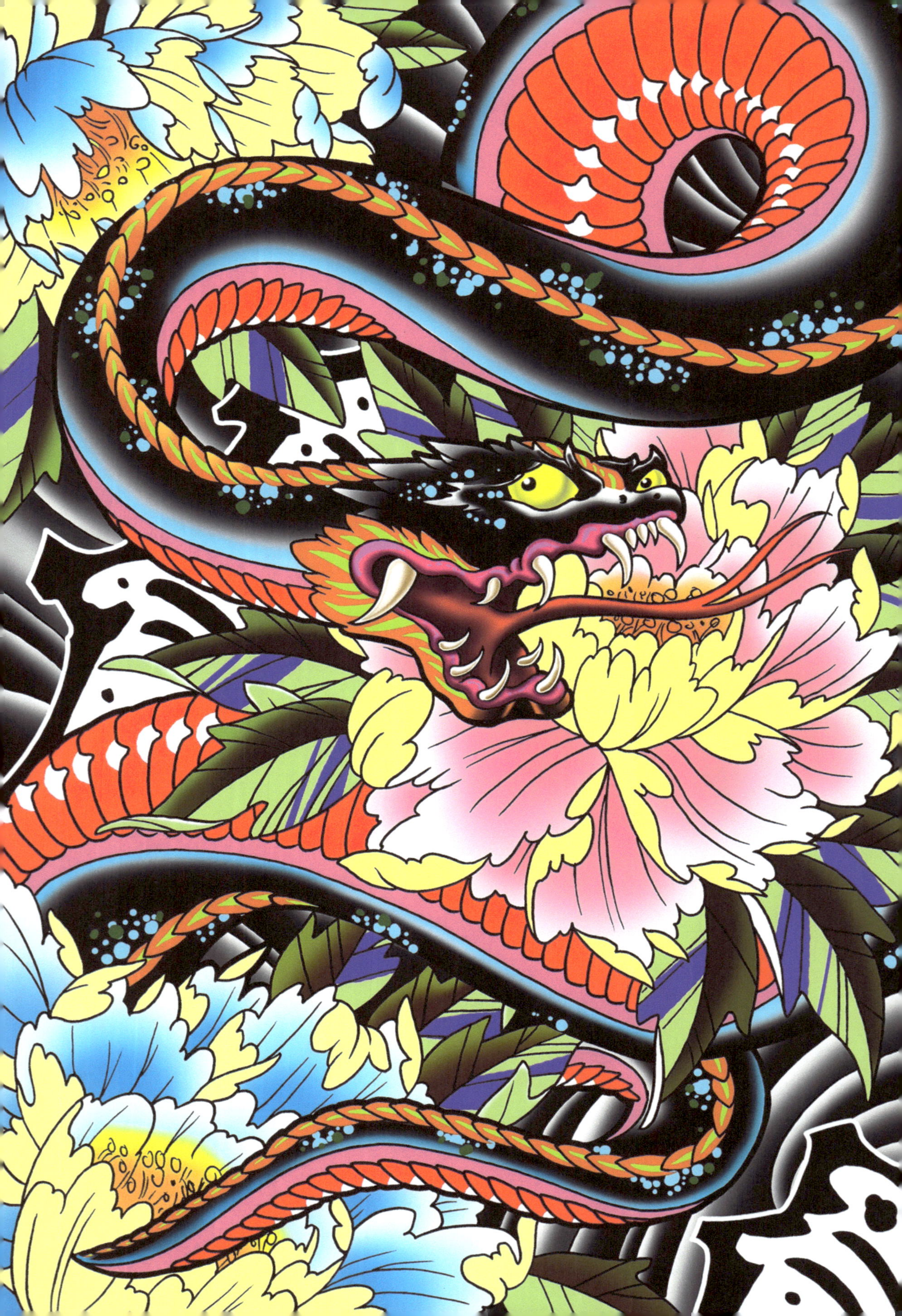

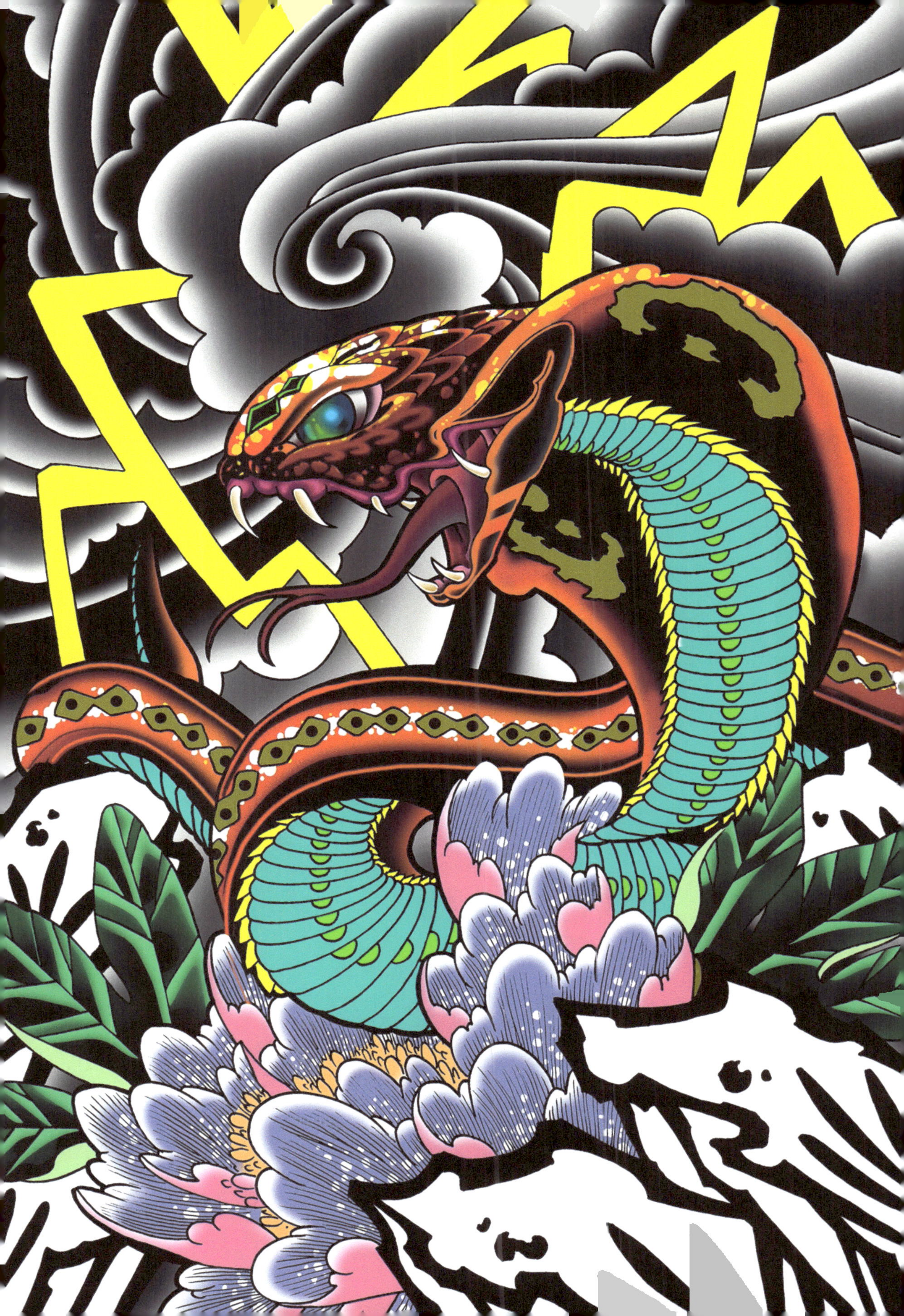

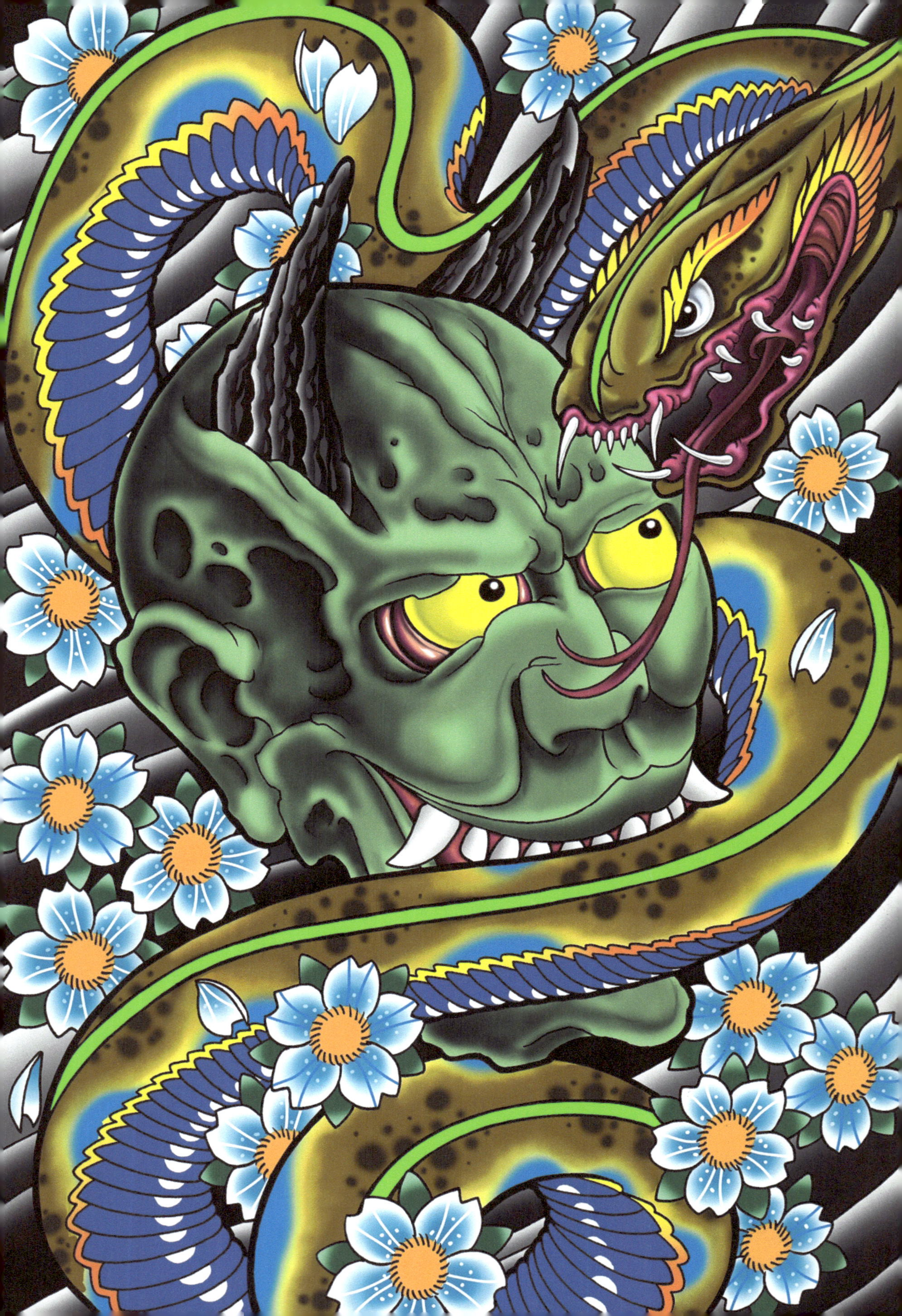

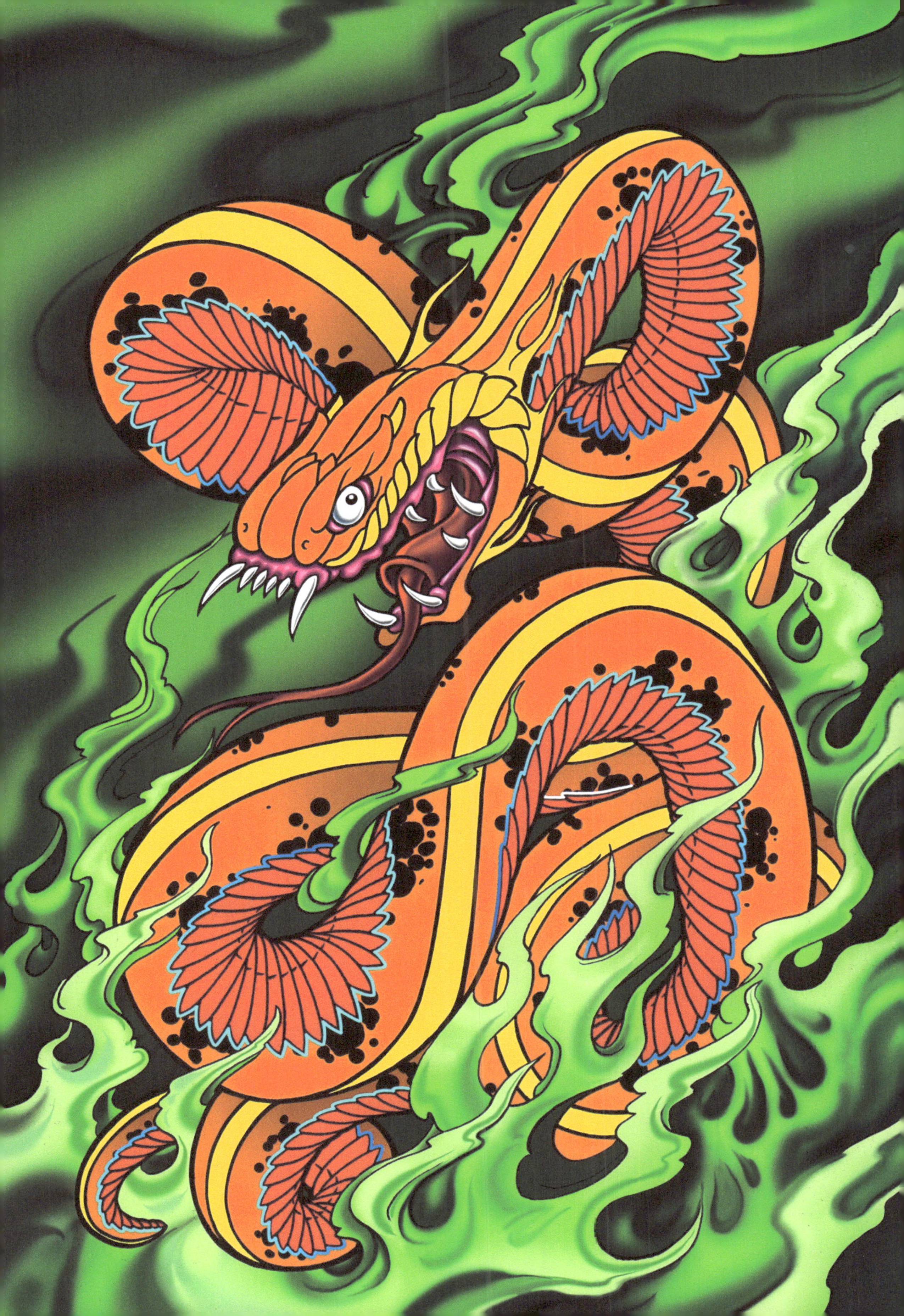

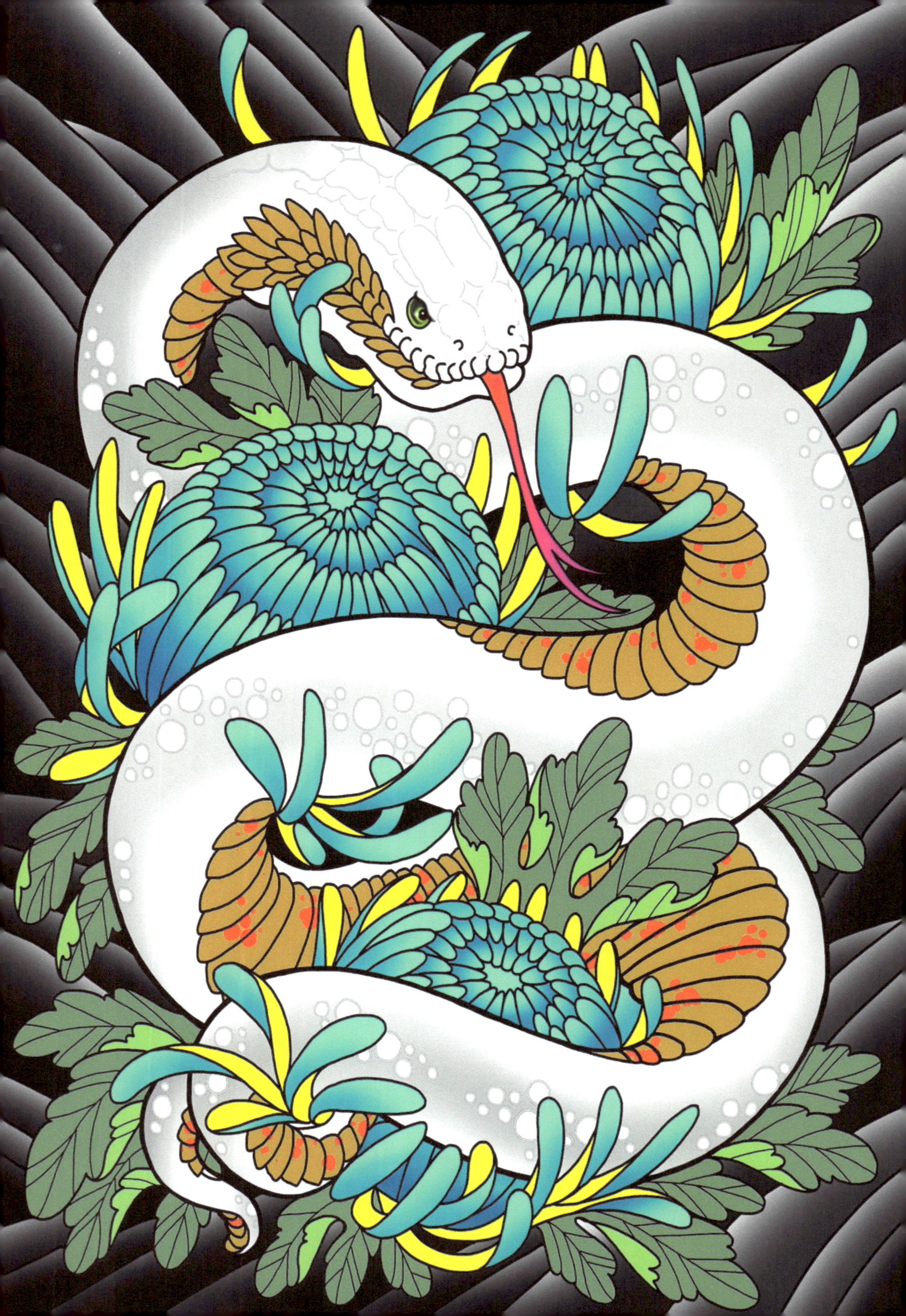

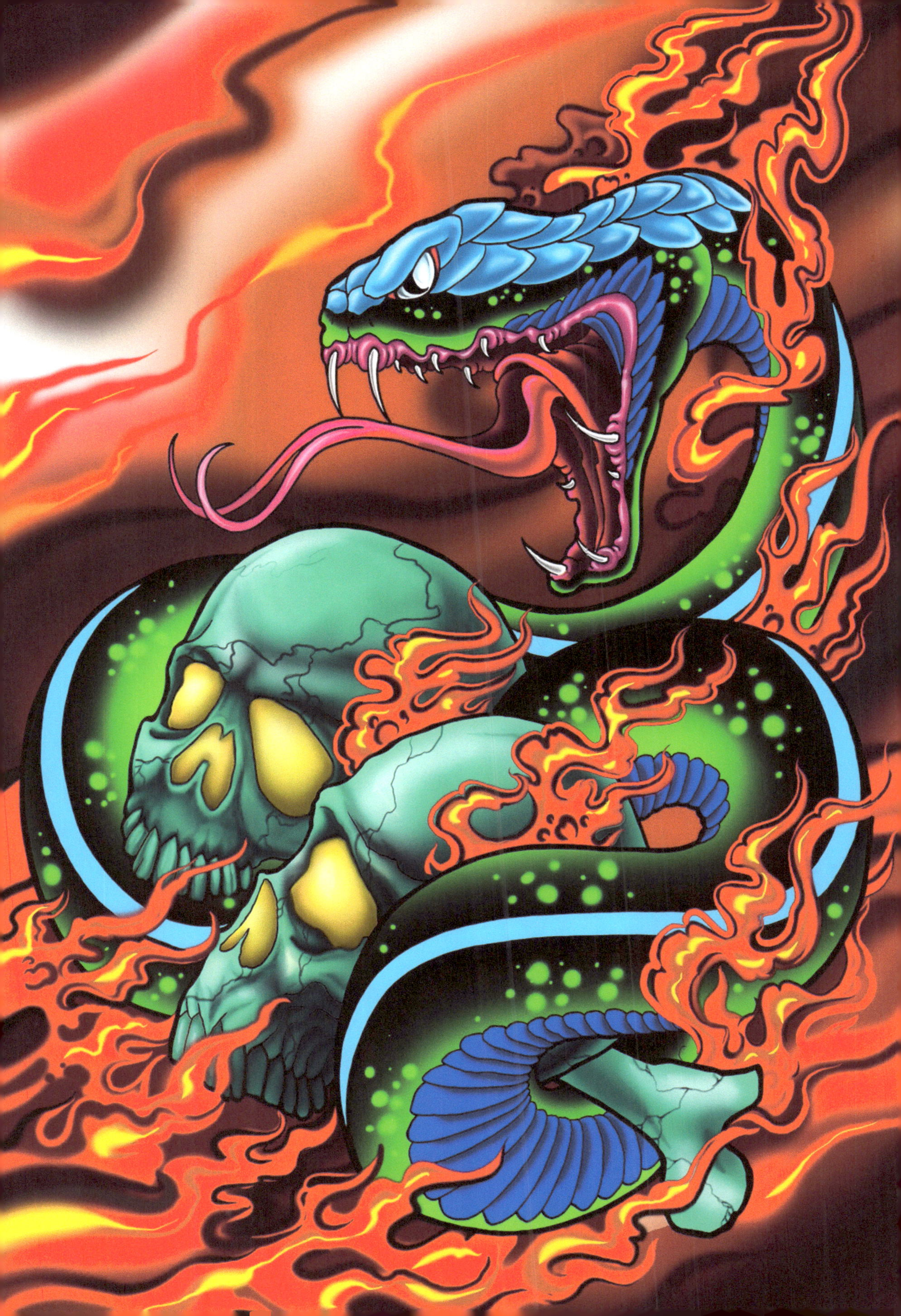

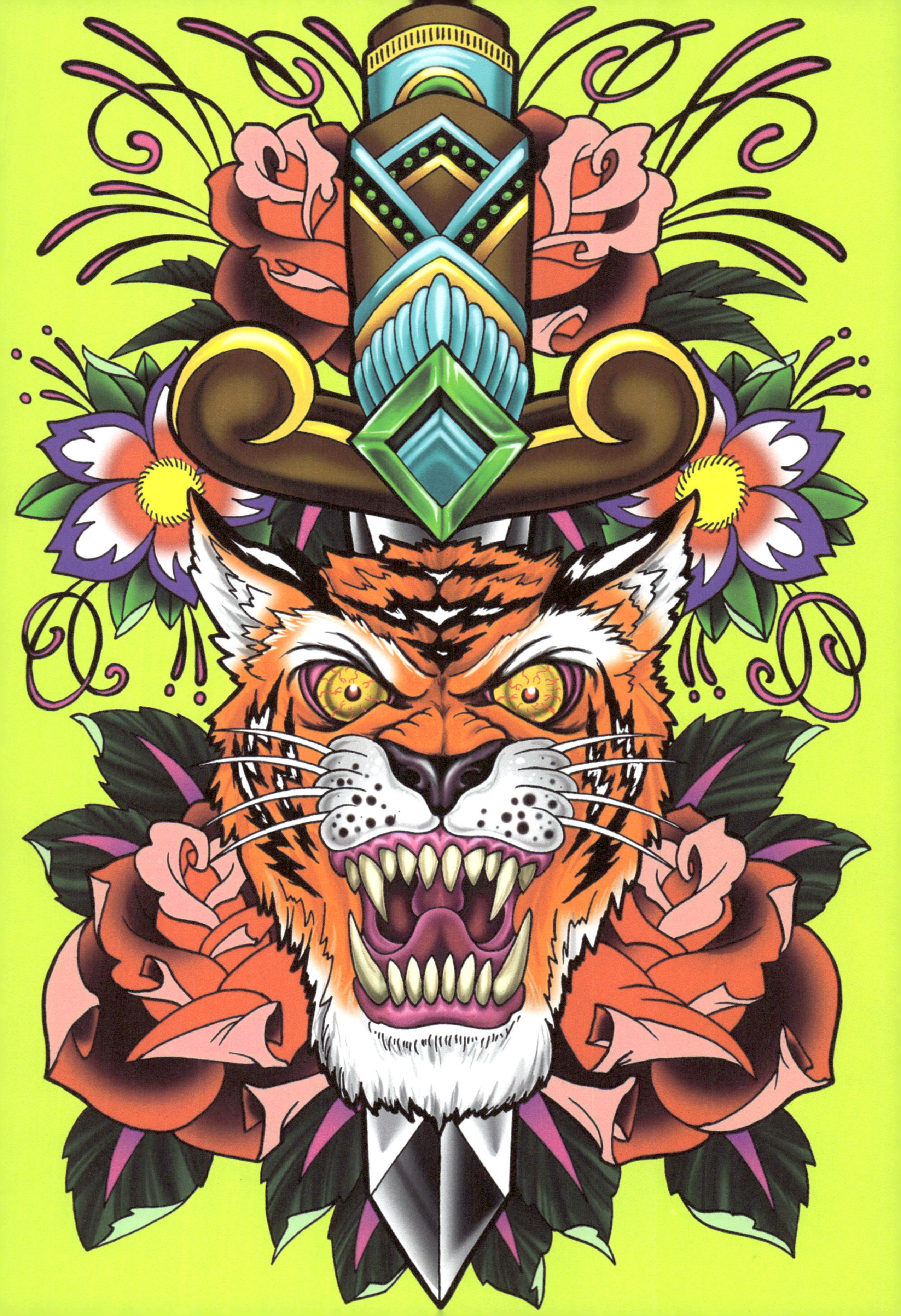

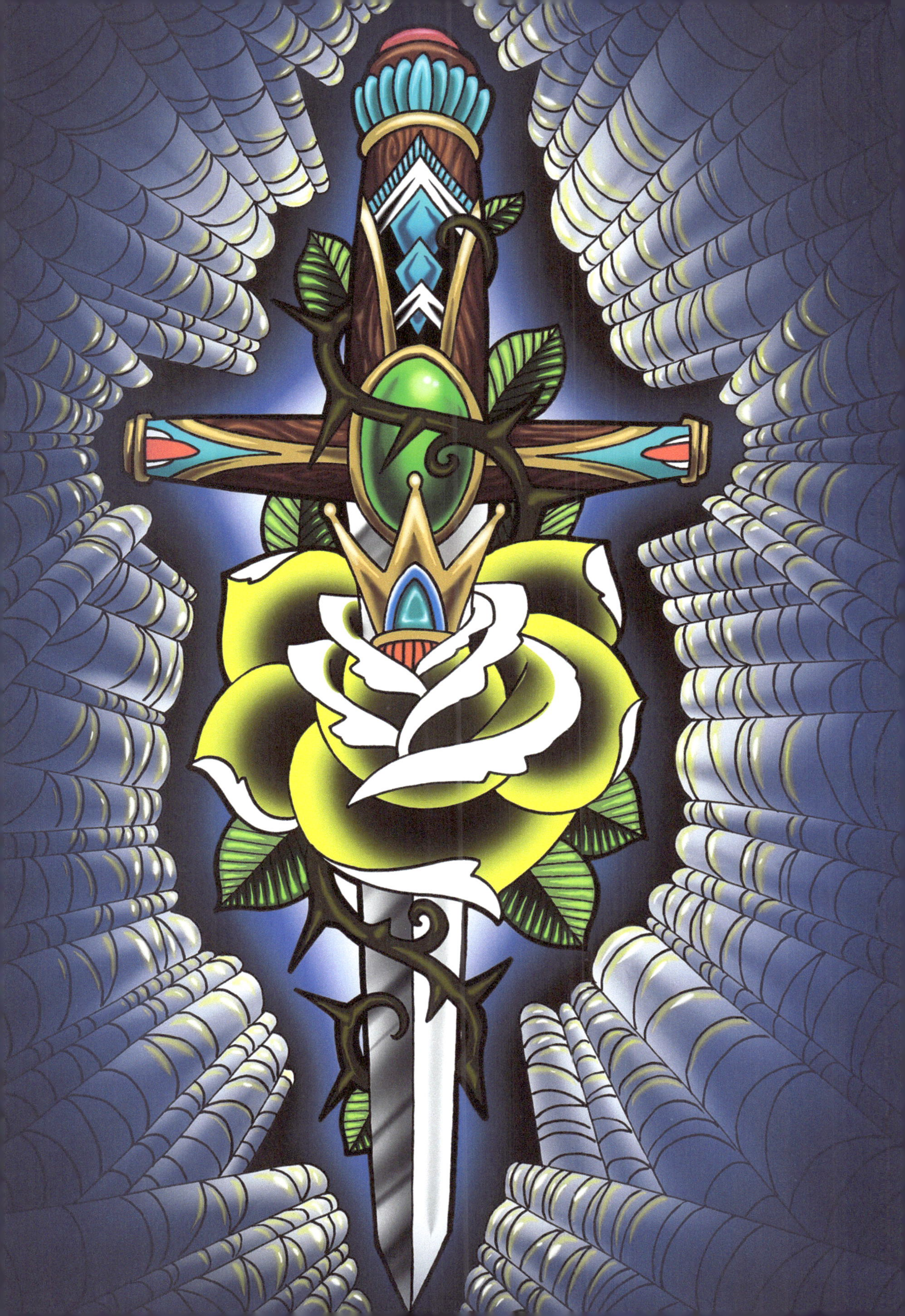

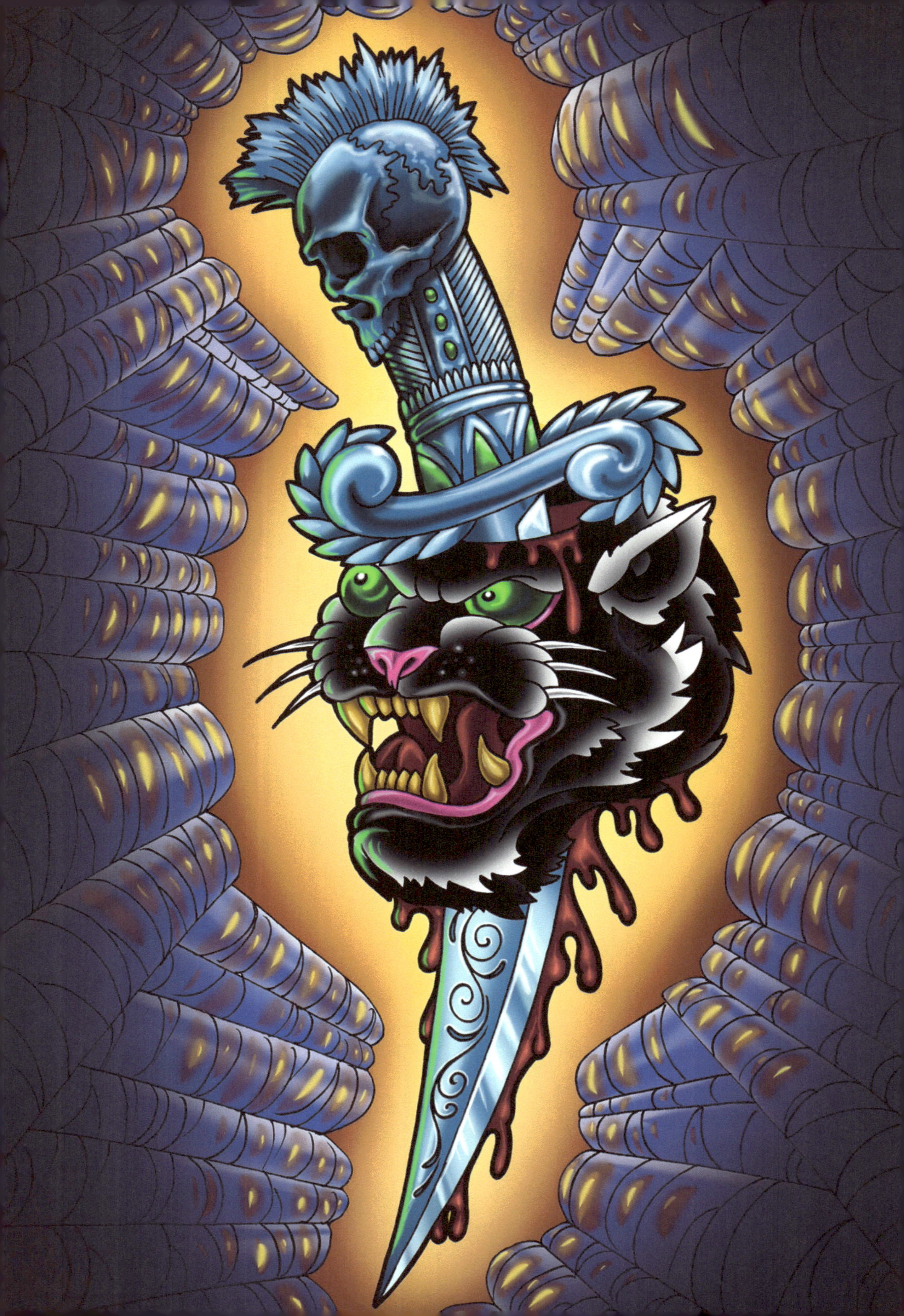

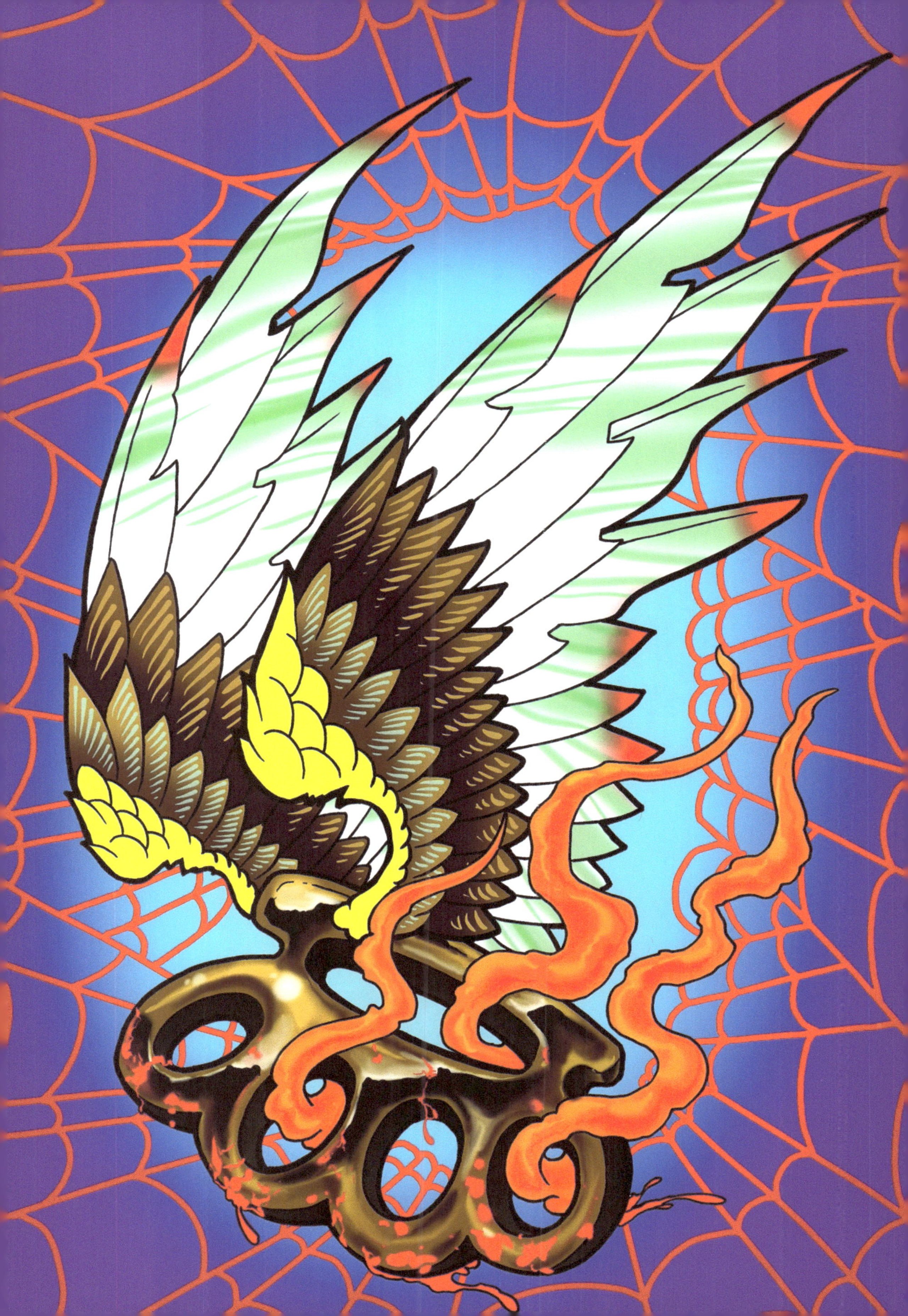

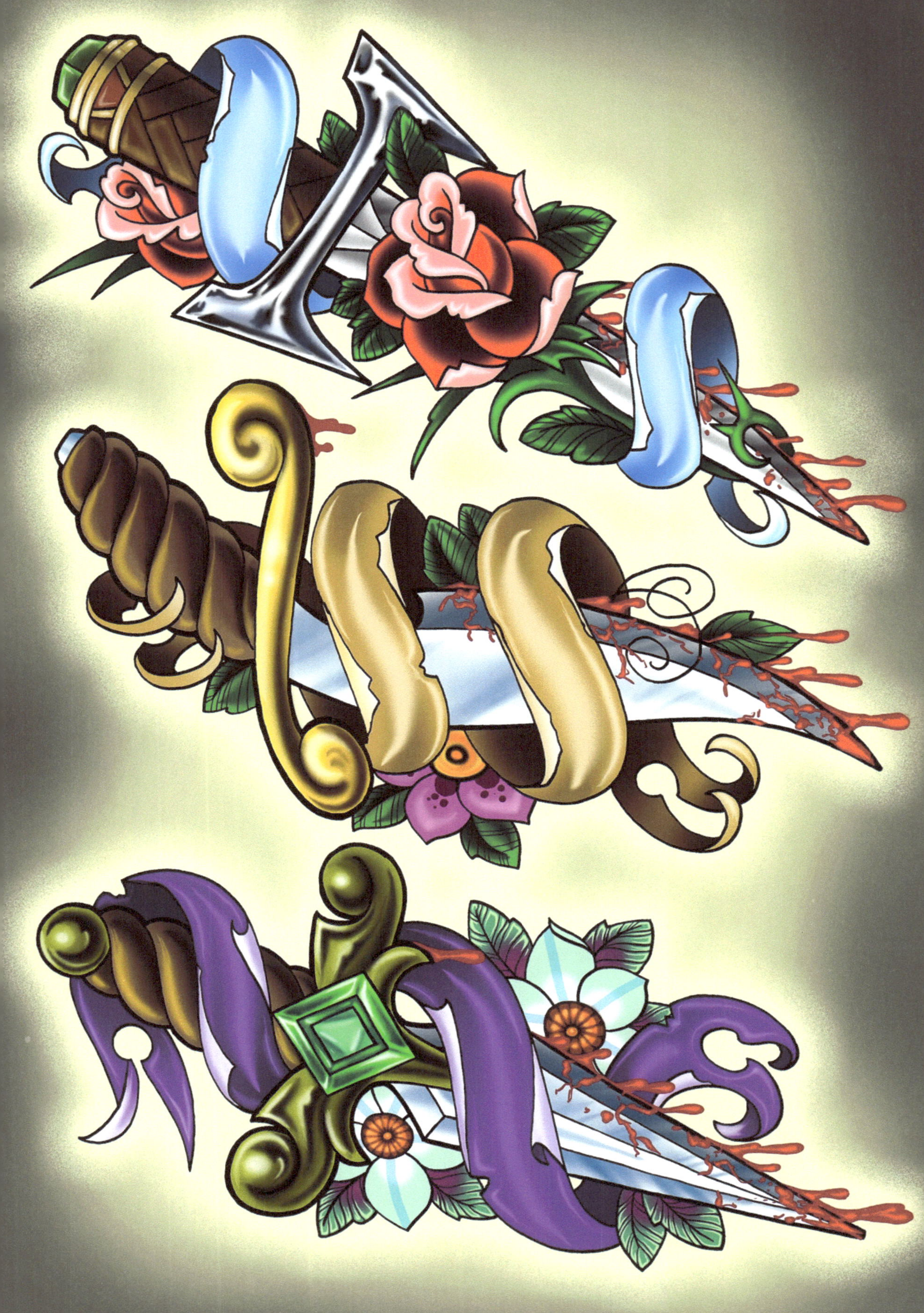

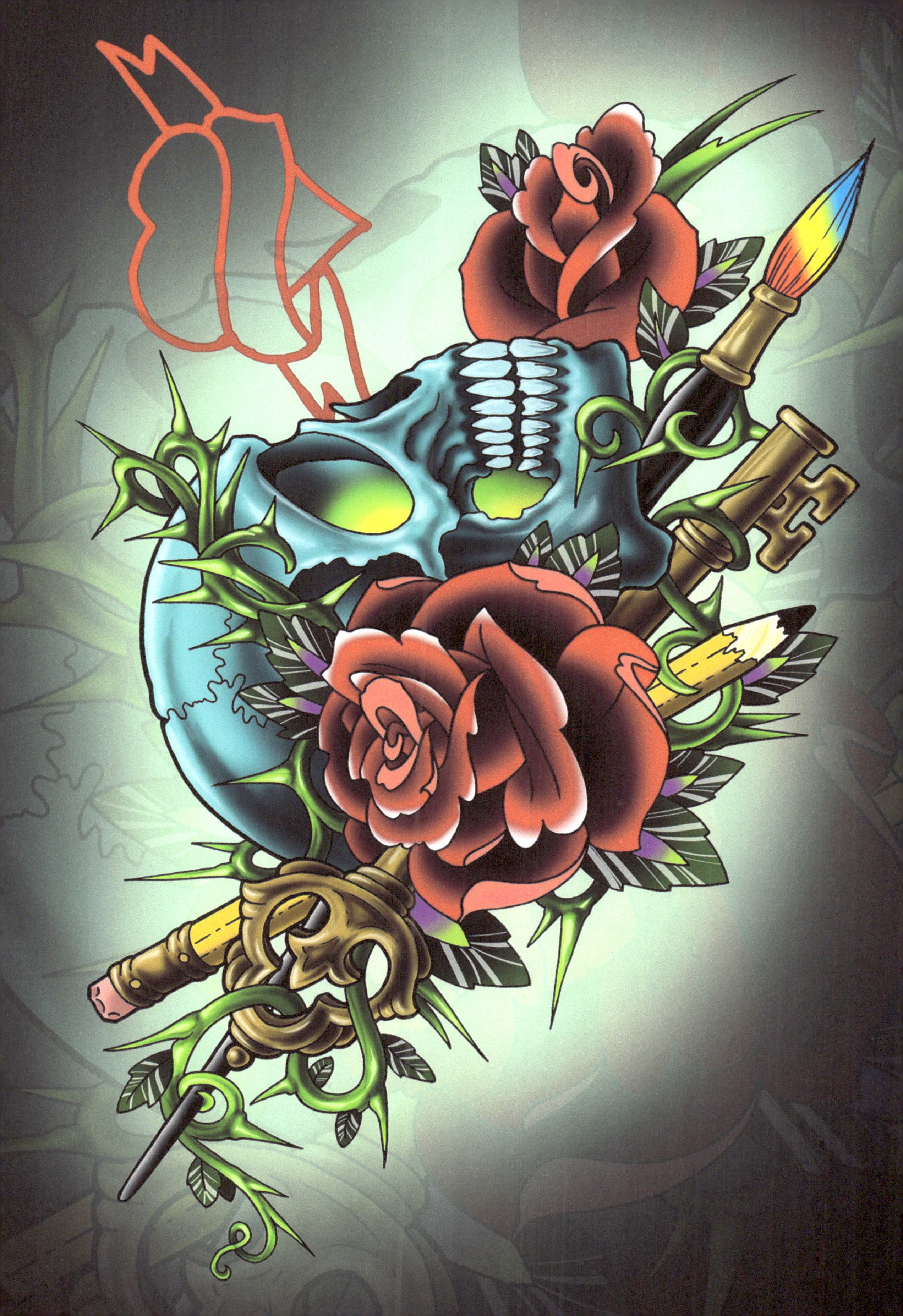

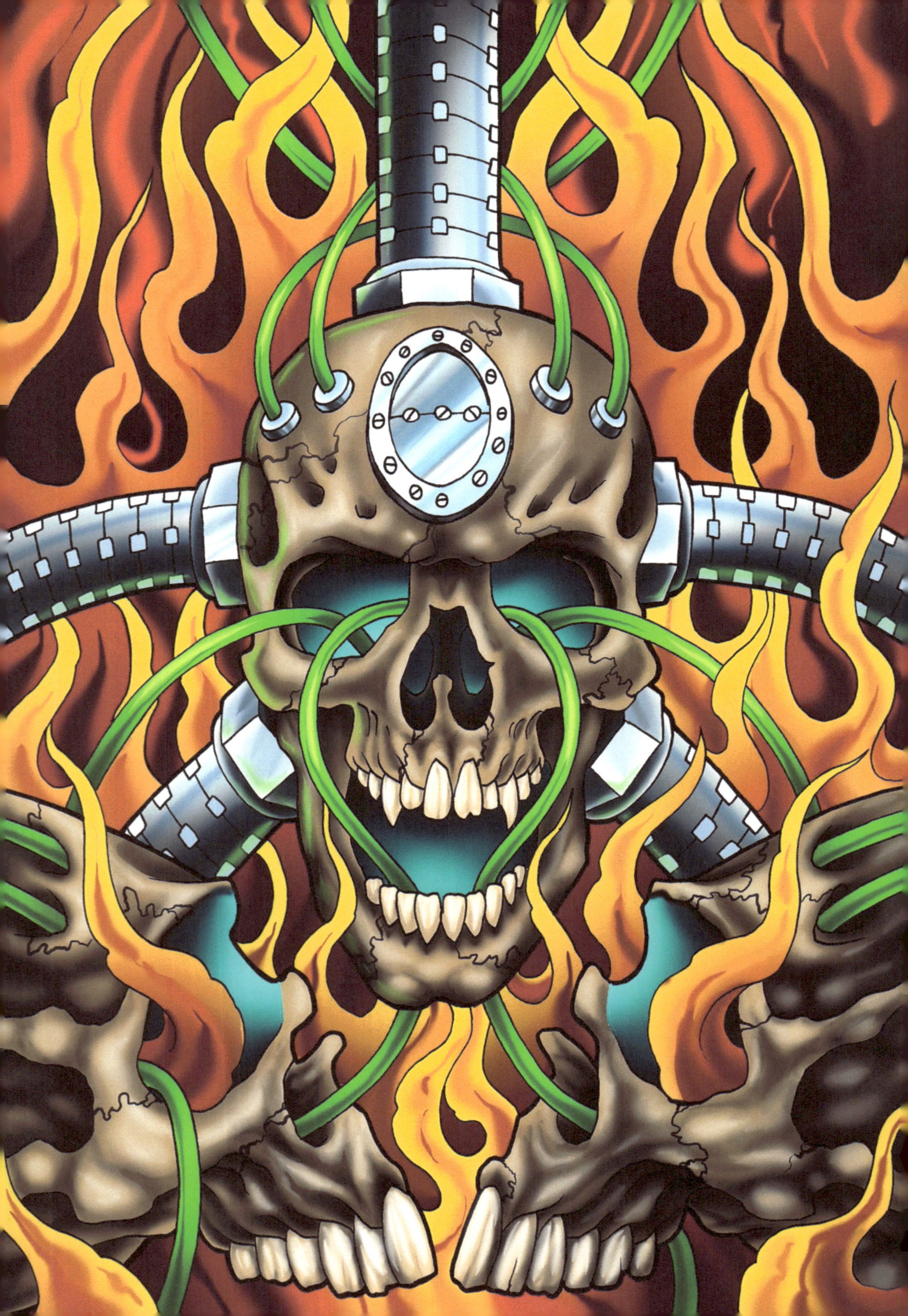

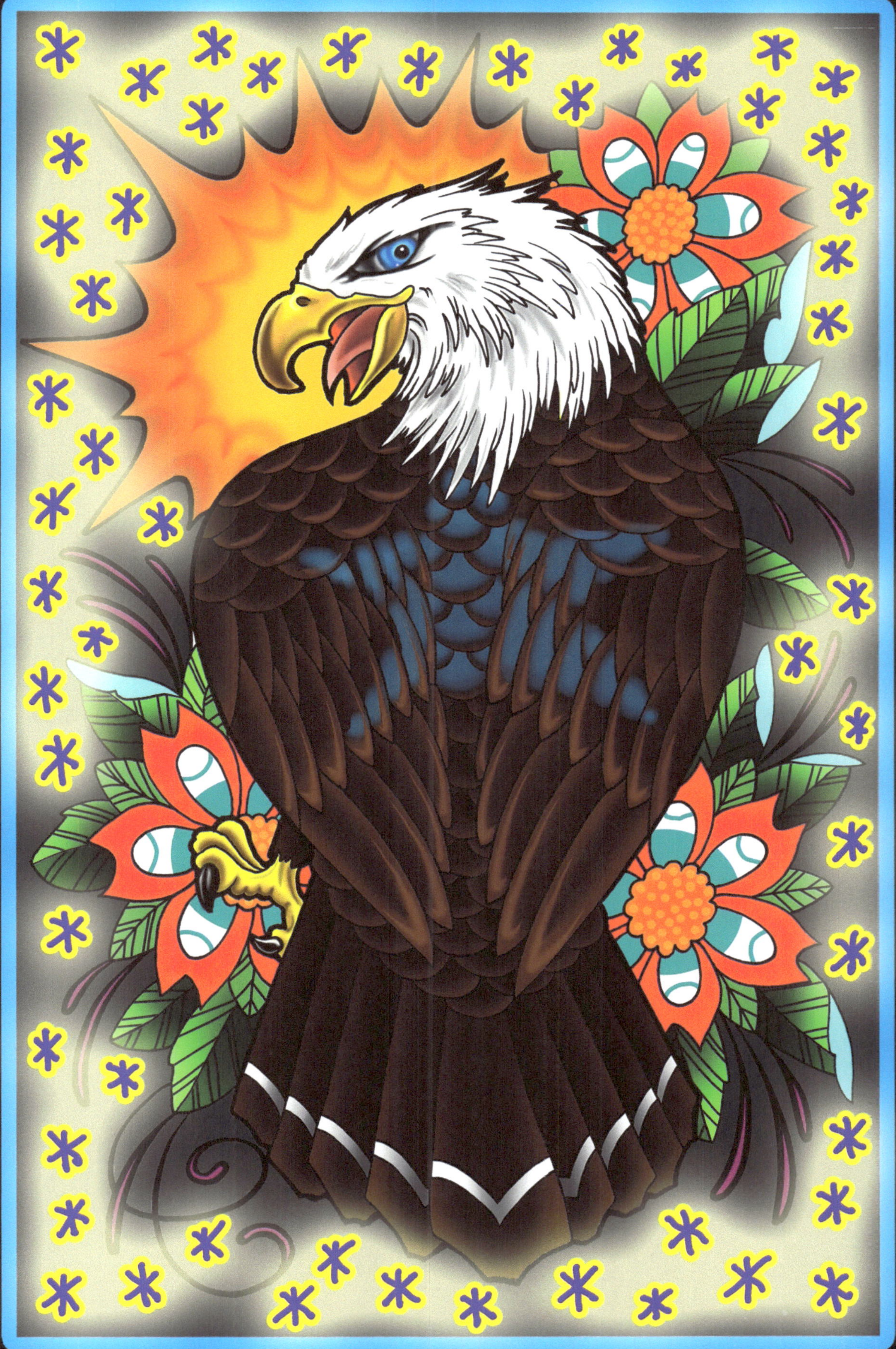

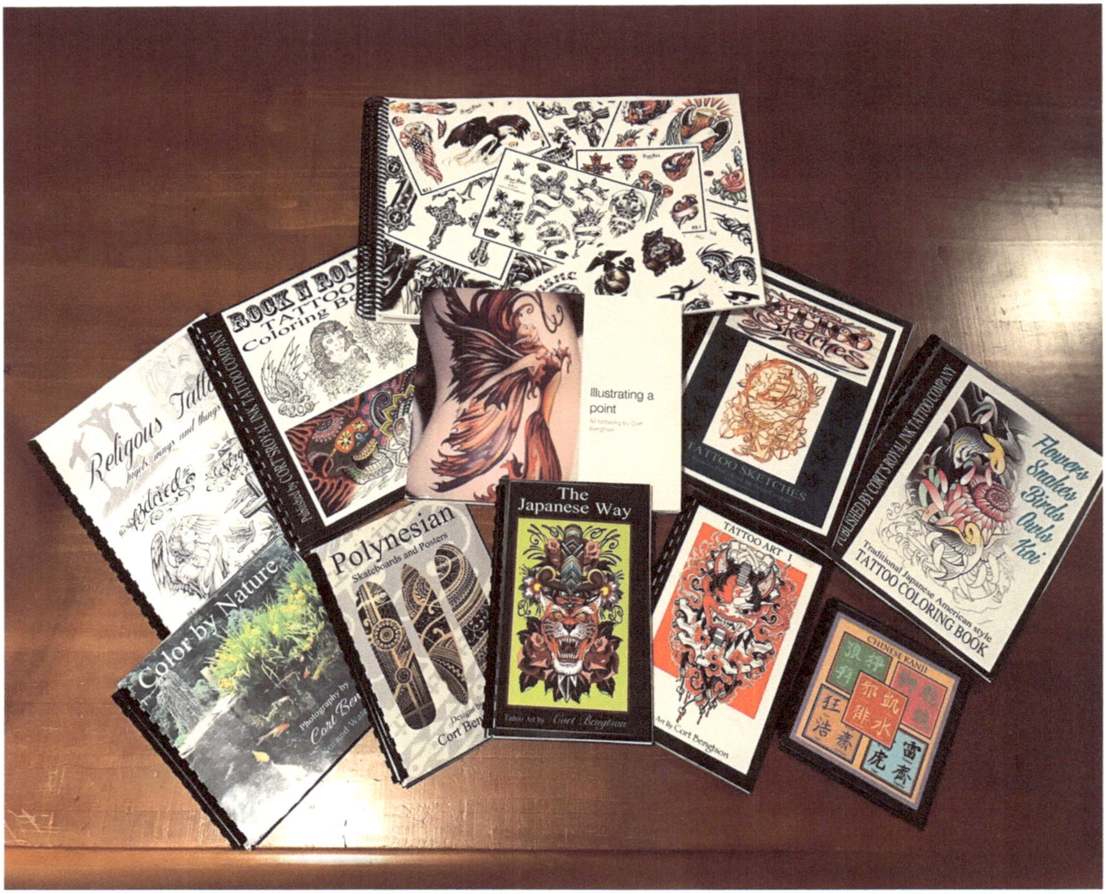

From Japanese style to surreal black and gray, to watercolors and computer art, we have something you will love. Prints ranging in size from 11" x 17" to 40" x 50" will adjust the visual appeal of any room.

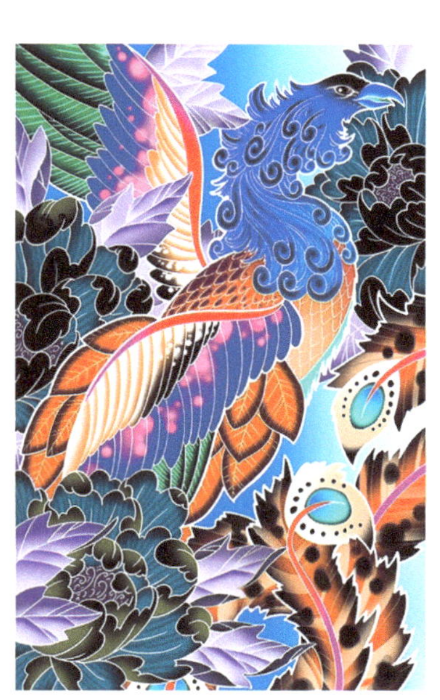

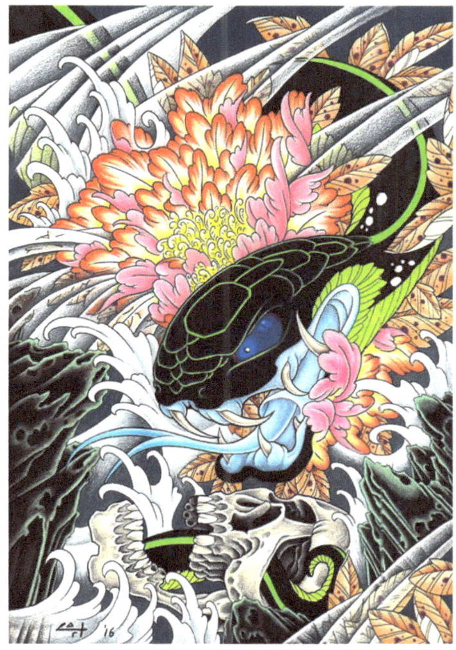

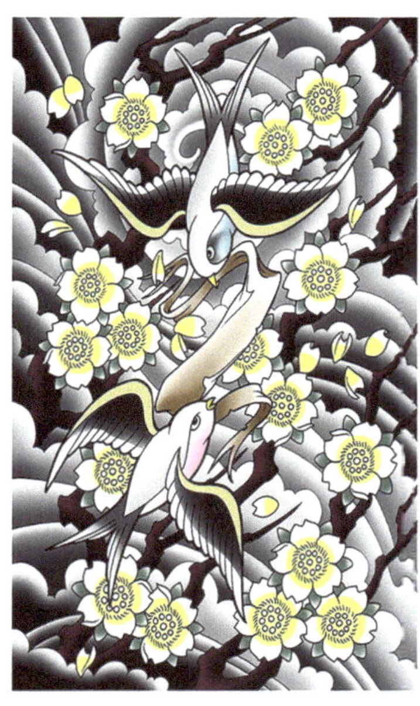

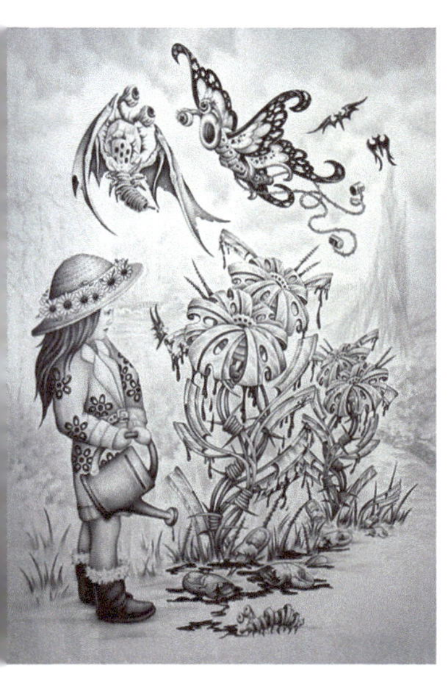

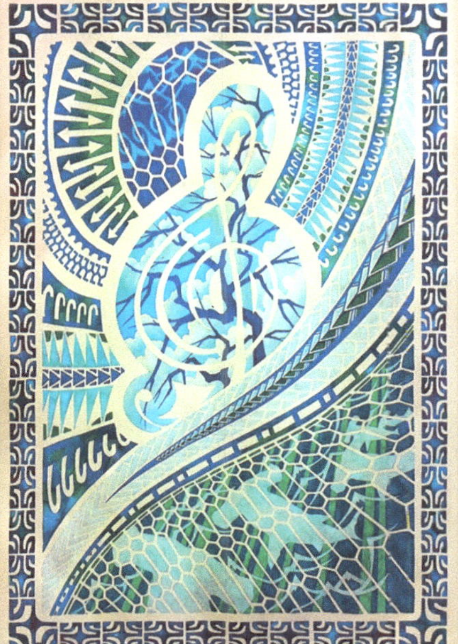

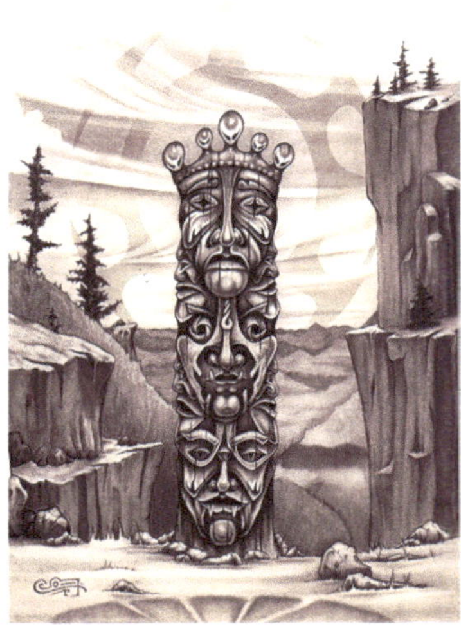

www.ingramcontent.com/pod-product-compliance
Lightning Source LLC
LaVergne TN
LVHW070217110826
845147LV00003B/592
* 9 7 8 1 9 4 8 1 8 7 0 3 9 *